Joint Penetration

Hot Under the Collar #3

Katherine McIntyre

Cover design by: Cate Ashwood Designs

http://www.cateashwooddesigns.com/

Editing: Tanja Ongkiehong

Printed in the United States of America

Contents

To my spouse, who's probably tired of having books dedicated to them...and yet I'm going to keep doing it anyway.

Acknowledgements

Ending a series is hard. I clearly wasn't ready to let go of this crew, which is why we're going to have a spinoff coming next—and of course there are ideas percolating for a spinoff of the spinoff. Ollie and Liam's story just poured out of me, like this whole trilogy did, and I was sad to see it finish, even though I loved writing it so much.

For Joint Penetration, I owe a huge thanks to Melissa, Nicole, and Julie for beta reading this book to make sure it closed out the series well. Of course, always a thanks to my author friends for letting me bounce ideas off them or simply gush over what my ridiculous characters are doing. A huge thanks as well to Cate Ashwood for knocking it out of the park with the cover and to Tanja for her sharp editorial skills.

I'm so, so grateful for my reader group and all of my wonderful readers. Your reception to this series made me so happy, and I loved the way you guys embraced the Hot Under the Collar crew.

And as always, a thank you to my wonderful friends and family for all the support and encouragement—I wouldn't be able to do any of this without you.

Chapter One

Liam

I hated parties.

Having people over wasn't high on my agenda, but part of the deal with having a highly extroverted roommate like Maeve and a tight-knit, needy friend group was that I ended up at something social most weekends. And since it was Maeve's birthday, I couldn't possibly get out of attending the cram-packed party at our apartment.

Maybe I could at least kick them out at nine.

"Look who just showed up," Rhys said, drawing my attention to the door.

I followed his gaze. In walked Theo with Lex, his new boyfriend, who he'd been denying dating until recently. The guys made a cute pair—Theo, a burly bear who wore the hell out of nice suits, and Lex, a tall, lanky charmer who wouldn't wear formalwear if his life depended on it. A smirk curled my lips. I'd seen that relationship a mile away, even if no one else had.

"I still can't wrap my brain around this," Cole said, rubbing his nape. "It's been a long-ass time since I've seen Lex look so settled down."

Rhys had drawn Cole into our merry band of friends, and with him had come his best friend, Lex, who'd snatched our forever unlucky-in-love Theo. Though it looked like his luck had finally changed.

"Daddy, I'm hungry," Sammy called to Rhys, kicking his little feet on the couch. The two-year-old was Rhys and Kelsey's son, the result of the two of them giving "best friends to lovers" a good old college try. Kelsey was happier in her triad with Marco and Ruby, while Rhys had met his match with Cole. They'd proved clear as day that best friends didn't just develop feelings after years of friendship.

No matter how much I wished it would happen.

I'd never admitted the words out loud, but Oliver Brannon was my first crush, and those stupid swoony butterflies had never gone away. No matter how many roadblocks stood in my way—especially the two biggest.

Straight.

Married.

Theo and Lex marched my way, and I couldn't hide my smirk. I adjusted my perch on the side of my couch, which I'd much rather be curled into while playing Final Fantasy 14, but we were apparently being social tonight, at least until I escaped to my bedroom to crash out.

Theo slipped over to me, his hand entwined with Lex's, and fuck, he looked so happy. His eyes were glowing, his expression light, and I couldn't be happier for him. Committed relationships might not be for me, but Theo had wanted one for so long, but instead of finding a good guy, he had only attracted shitheads. Our entire friend group had breathed a sigh of relief to see him with someone who cared.

I'd had one far-too-long stint with a shithead, and that had soured me on the whole deal for good.

I had hookups, and I had Ollie. Both my needs for sex and camaraderie were filled, so why change a solid thing?

The door to our apartment flung open, and as if summoned by thought alone, Ollie stormed in.

My big bear of a best friend was burly in the best ways, with a light, trimmed beard and tattoos and gauges. Fuck, I lost my mind over all three of those things. He'd tossed on a black tee and wrinkled flannel, and his tight jeans might have been distracting if I hadn't seen his expression. Ollie was brightness incarnate, one of those guys with the booming laughs that made you feel warm just by being in his presence.

Except today, he looked devastated.

Dark circles were under his deep brown eyes, and his haunted expression had my internal alarms clanging.

I missed what Maeve asked Ollie, but I definitely didn't miss my best friend's next statement as he marched into the house.

"I need to drink tonight. Josie wants a divorce."

Divorce.

Ollie was getting divorced.

I sat frozen, not believing my ears as Ollie headed toward the kitchen where we kept the booze. Theo jostled my shoulder.

"Go get him."

Theo passed me a meaningful look. If anyone would've pieced together my crush, it would've been him.

"Right," I said, rising from the couch and all but floating toward the kitchen. Ollie clanked around with bottles and hadn't even looked my way, but that didn't matter. I needed to be by his side.

My chest squeezed tight at the memory of when he'd first told me he and Josie were going to get married. They'd been fighting a lot our senior year of high school, and I was going away for college, so I had been about to spill my guts. To tell Ollie how I felt.

Except he'd interrupted with the three words that wrecked me to this day. "Josie said yes."

I stepped onto the tiled floor of the kitchen, the rest of the apartment in view due to the open layout, yet I felt worlds away from everyone at the party. Ollie looked up at me, and the devastation in his expression had me racing to close the space between us. Any thoughts flew out the window as I threw my arms around him and plastered myself to his chest. Ollie smelled like a mix of metal and patchouli that always felt warm and familiar to me, and even though he sagged into my tight hold, I soaked in the comfort of him.

"Left field, huh?" I murmured against his shoulder.

He pulled away but kept a grip on my arm and let out a shaky sigh. Ollie tried to force a grin because of course the cheerful asshole did. "I mean, she wasn't cheating on me at least."

"One up on Patti Lennon, then," I responded, my lip quirking the slightest bit.

"Wow, my judgment's vastly improved since sophomore year of high school," Ollie muttered, dripping sarcasm. "Now come help me make a drink. I don't think I put the right ratio in."

"You never do." I shook my head. He'd pulled out a bottle of Triple Sec, gin, and vermouth. No mixers in sight. So damn typical. "Out of the way." I muscled past him and pushed the empty glass away from whatever nightmare he prepared to pour into the cup. Ever since our senior year of high school, when Ollie made a concoction of tequila, red wine, and Mountain Dew that ended the party with everyone puking their guts up, I'd been designated his official bartender.

Ollie moved right next to me, heat rolling off him as he loomed by my side. I sucked in a sharp breath and tried to summon sad thoughts to tamp down the stirring of my cock. Ollie's divorce wasn't doing the trick, because the minuscule hope I'd been repressing ever since we met in the first week of our freshman year of high school sparked to life with the fervor of a cheerleader on meth.

I grabbed the rum and ginger ale from our makeshift bar—aka, the huddle of bottles along the back of the counter. In a few quick motions, I poured the shots of rum and filled the rest up with ginger ale, all while Ollie stared at me with an intensity that had always weakened my knees.

"So, what happened?" I asked, trying to distract myself from the fucking flutters in my chest. Knowing a divorce was on the table had cracked open the box I'd locked my crush into years ago, and I was fucking buzzing.

Ollie heaved a sigh and leaned against the kitchen counter. Maeve shouted from the other side of the room, but she was loud by default, so I didn't bother glancing in her direction. No, my gaze locked and loaded on my best friend as I passed over the drink, my hand surprisingly steady.

"She got this job offer for a senior-level marketing position in her company." He took a sip from the glass. "Fuck, you make good drinks. Anyway, she accepted it without even talking to me. Despite the fact that my whole family's here, our business is here, whatever. She said she thought we got married too young, and she needed a chance to fucking find herself." He glanced away, not meeting my gaze.

"Well, shit." I licked my lips. I needed to approach this one carefully. Did I think they'd gotten married too young? Well, yeah. Given the amount of fights they'd had through the years, even post marriage, they'd never felt like a good fit. But I was biased as hell. I'd always had a stupid thing for my very straight best friend, who still wouldn't be looking my way with any interest now that he was single. I was setting myself up for more heartbreak.

I mean, if I had a cold, dead little heart to break. Feelings only happened on Tuesday evenings, which I reserved for playing Final Fantasy.

"Were you guys fighting more or anything?" I wrinkled my nose. My hands started moving on their own volition as I made a rum and ginger ale for myself. I would need it tonight.

"That's the weird part," Ollie said, raking his fingers through his thick, dark strands. "We'd barely been fighting all year."

I arched a brow. "I'd say that's the weirder part." Ollie was one of the smartest fucking people I knew when it came to anything practical, working with his hands, piecing fixtures together, but my god, he couldn't read people worth a shit. His fights with Josie had been steady through the thirteen years of their relationship, so for them to all of a sudden have smooth sailing would've been a massive blinking signal something wasn't right.

Ollie tipped back his drink, and just like that, half of it vanished.

"Oh, so it's one of those nights?" I asked, trying to keep the mood lighter for him. If he needed to sob into my shoulder, he could, and if he needed to blow up things, I was game.

If he needed to fuck his feelings out, hell, my ass would be on offer so fast it was ridiculous, but that was a fantasy that would never come true.

"I'm pretty sure impending divorce ranks pretty high on reasons to drink," Ollie said, running his thumb over his lush lower lip, which glistened from the liquid. I swallowed hard, trying to tamp down the rampant lust I had for my best friend. If he wasn't stupidly hot, funny as fuck, and the easiest person in the world to be around, it might be easier.

"So, Josie's moving away?" I took a sip of my drink while casually leaning against the counter.

Ollie hissed. "Don't say her name, Liam. That's like rule number one of ex-wives, right?"

A snort escaped me. "What, like she's Beetlejuice or something? Recite three times, and she's summoned?"

"Look, I don't make the rules," Ollie said, scrubbing his face. My palms itched as I restrained myself from grabbing his hands to keep him from doing the motion again. I hated seeing him this distraught, but I'd be lying if a part of me wasn't relieved. He and Josie had never been a great fit, clear by the amount they disagreed, but they'd leaped headfirst into marriage and tried to make it work for years.

"Okay, bitches, it's cupcake time," Maeve called in her bull-horn-like voice, loud enough to wake the dead.

"Why don't you have a cupcake? Divorce rule number two, binge on sugar." I placed my hand on Ollie's low back and steered him toward the dining room, where everyone had gathered around the table. At least, those who weren't sitting on the couches. We had a regular-sized two-bedroom apartment and not enough room for our growing number of friends. The obvious solution would be to off them one by one and stage a murder mystery, since our friends loved games.

Might be a little morbid, but working as a PT for so long had clearly affected me.

"I'm not above eating pity cupcakes and getting trashed tonight, but you better be prepared for me to crash here," Ollie said as we joined the others so we could sing happy birthday to Maeve. She was in her element with the people crammed into our apartment, and as much as I whined about crowds, seeing her at her prime, all pure energy and excitement, was always awesome. Her ear-length, flame-red hair matched the equally loud green dress she wore, like she repped Christmas real hard, despite it being summer.

Ollie and I wedged ourselves into a spot at the table. "Like you don't crash here most of the time anyway?" Whenever we pulled late nights, Ollie stayed over, which I fucking loved. Our friendship had always been like that, with us in each other's pockets—at least until he got engaged and I headed across the state for college. However, when I moved back to the area, we'd picked up our friendship like nothing had changed. And maybe it hadn't been the sign of health for his relationship that he never seemed too eager to get home to Josie, but I wasn't complaining.

"You've got a comfy couch," he said with a shrug.

The "Happy Birthday" song kicked in, and Ollie and I joined into the fray, our friends getting louder with each verse if that were humanly possible. Sammy let out an excited shriek, and Maeve scooped him up to let him blow out the candle on her cupcake. My heart squeezed tight at the sight of everyone here, at the makeshift family of friends we'd somehow cobbled together. Ollie bumped his shoulder against mine, and I leaned against him.

Sure, the thought of us standing here as part of a couple made my chest ache something fierce, but I'd reconciled long ago that fantasy would never become true.

Ollie might be single now, but that didn't make him queer. Besides, I'd left the idea of relationships behind. Sure, Ollie was the one man on this planet who could make me reconsider, but that was as likely to happen as the Pope doing a striptease.

"Get your cupcake, Hunger Games style," Maeve called out, snagging two cupcakes, one for her and one for Sammy, before bolting away with the kiddo. Everyone dove in at once and grabbed the lemon and vanilla cupcakes Theo had made for her. The man could *bake*, so I wouldn't pass up on a chance at his cupcakes. Still, I wasn't in any rush to pull myself away from Ollie. The feel of his big body against mine and the heat emanating from him lured me in, and I'd hold on to it for as long as I could.

Finally, he took a cupcake as well, and I followed suit.

The party had returned to the living room, but the kitchen was still fairly empty.

I nudged him in the side. "Want another drink?"

"Are you trying to get me drunk, Liam Kelly?" Ollie said, his tone lighter than it had been all evening. I'd distract him for as long as he needed to stave away the pain.

"Tonight calls for Karaoke Drunk."

"Oh, fuck," he said, letting out a low whistle. "That's some sort of legendary. How many drinks will it take to get you to belt out Queen again?"

I winked and blew a kiss. "Let's find out?"

Time to drink hard enough to forget I had a raging crush on my now-single best friend.

Chapter Two

Ollie

My eyes felt glued shut, and my throat was dry as fuck.

Slowly I blinked and blinked again. I wasn't in my house, but I'd apparently made it to a bed. However, before I sat up, the memories of everything that had happened yesterday slammed into me, keeping my head firmly on the pillow.

Josie's solemn face. The casual way she'd dropped the word *divorce* like a bomb and how my body disintegrated in the aftermath.

Tearing out of my house like it had caught on fire to escape the reality that everything was about to change.

Showing up at Liam's and drinking my face off.

A rendition of Fat Bottomed Girls that Liam had tweaked to Fat Bottomed Guys.

I pressed my palm to my forehead and let out a groan, shocked I didn't have more of a hangover. The empty glass of water and empty

Tylenol wrapper on the nightstand explained why. Someone had been smart last night, and I didn't think it happened to be me.

A slight snore penetrated my foggy brain, and a heavy arm rested around my waist, a body plastered behind mine. I peered over my shoulder. Liam was curled up behind me, strands of his dirty blond hair askew and his eyelashes looking impossibly long. His chest moved up and down with his steady breaths in slumber, and I gripped on to the sense of peace that brought—mostly because I knew it would get shattered the moment I got up to face the day.

We hadn't slept in the same bed in ages, so this vaulted me right back to high school when that had been the norm. Ever since Liam had returned to the area after college, I'd crashed at his place countless times, but I always slept on the couch or the floor, depending on how shitfaced I'd gotten or tired I was.

I shifted to a seated position, which caused his arm to drift back onto the bed. The loss of contact sucked, though. When I was hurting, I turned into a fucking puppy, constantly needing physical touch. Or to fuck, but considering my divorce, I wouldn't be getting laid anytime soon. I wrinkled my nose as I looked down at my chest—my bare chest.

Had I stripped down last night? I tossed the sheets off, accidentally dragging them off Liam. I was wearing boxer briefs still, so I hadn't hopped into bed buck naked with my best friend. Not like Liam would've judged.

My gaze snagged on Liam next to me and held.

He must've also ditched the clothes last night, but he wasn't wearing boxer briefs.

Purple panties.

My mouth dried, and I couldn't look away, even though I should. With the way he sprawled on his side, his legs slightly spread, the satin front barely cupped his prominent erection and the lace back that offered minimal coverage for his ass cheeks. Holy hell. I knew Liam had a pretty nice ass, but god*damn*. His ass cheeks were two perfect round globes accentuated by the purple lace, the color contrasting his pale skin all too well.

My morning wood strained my boxer briefs, but the zing of lust was undeniable.

Well, damn. That was a new one.

Liam shifted with a few snuffles and a low groan that went straight to my balls. Apparently, getting divorced had sent me to new levels of horny. Not like I didn't know Liam was an attractive guy, with his soulful blue eyes, dirty blond hair that always seemed slightly tousled, and a slim, muscular body from years of running. I just wasn't used to getting an instant reaction over him.

Granted, in our seventeen years of friendship, I'd also never seen him stripped down to purple panties either.

Fucking eye-opener that was.

I pressed at my cock, willing it to calm down. Instead, the needy fucker took the touch as a sign I was about to get frisky, and a bit of pre-cum oozed from the head, imprinting on my boxer briefs.

"Nghrf," Liam mumbled as he flopped onto his stomach, placing his ass on clear display. I'd gotten an eyeful earlier, but this view—fu-uuuuck.

I licked my lips but then tore my gaze away from my best friend, who I shouldn't be ogling while he was asleep. Clearly, the divorce with Josie was messing with my head—both of them.

"Wait, why are you in my bed?" Liam asked as he pushed up beside me.

"The better question is how much did we drink last night?" I gestured at my bare chest.

Liam's cheeks pinked as he looked down—to those skimpy purple panties that honestly were fucking criminal. His whole body locked up, and panic flashed in his bright blue eyes. Oh, hell no. No awkwardness was allowed between us.

I tugged at the waistband of his panties. "When the hell did you start wearing sexy underwear?" I complained, stampeding on through the elephant in the room. "I feel like that's something your best friend should know."

Liam peered up at me, his gaze intense as hell, the pupils blown out. I pretty much leaned half over him, my finger hooked into the waistband of his panties. We both froze.. How could I backtrack from this situation without making it more awkward? My cock was definitely paying attention, testing the fabric of my boxer briefs, which was a weird-as-fuck experience, considering I'd been married as of yesterday.

Granted, the past year had been...well, Sahara-dry in the sex department.

And Liam's heavy breaths were distracting as fuck. His skin was hot to the touch, and I'd become a bit too aware of our proximity.

"Best friends don't need to share underwear preferences," he said, his voice coming out hoarse and low.

"Well, maybe we should. Look, I'm just wearing plain old boxer briefs to this party. An embarrassment."

Maybe mentioning my underwear had been a mistake. Liam raked his gaze down over my body slow, slow, slower, and the heat flaring in his eyes was unmistakable. He'd complimented my muscles before, and he didn't think I was ugly or anything, but a look that scorching? How the hell had I gone from finding out Josie was divorcing me yesterday to lying half-naked in my best friend's bed today?

The bigger question was why didn't I feel more broken up about losing Josie?

Unfortunately, the answer to that percolated in my gut, one I wasn't ready to face yet.

"Okay, we can stop comparing underwear," Liam said. I thought I'd seen every variant of Liam Kelly over the years, but this husky voice was new. Before I could think about it further, he knocked my hand away from his waistband. I responded on reflex, giving his chest a playful shove.

"Seriously, Ollie?" Liam exclaimed, thwacking me back in the chest. Something light and bubbly burst inside me.

"You want to do this?" I bumped him in the side with my shoulder. Except with my height and weight, I knocked him flat on his back.

"You fucker." Liam threw his whole body into me. The thump echoed around the room, and a bright grin spread on my face.

"Guess we're doing this," I said, launching full force at him, dropping my weight onto him like we were still teenagers and not thirty.

"Hey!" Liam knocked into me, sending me off balance and onto my side, but I dove in to try and reclaim the high ground. For a few moments, it was just thumps, heavy breaths, and scrambling for purchase as I tried to tug Liam back under me while he struggled to do the same. I fucking loved losing my head into something as simple and ridiculous as this, the years and complications melting away. Finally, I swung around on top, my legs on either side of his, and pinned his arms into the mattress.

Except he was writhing beneath me in nothing but those stupidly hot purple panties.

All of a sudden, our wrestling felt a *lot* different.

Liam and I were barely wearing anything, and I pinned him down with my weight, skin to skin. Hell, he emanated so much heat, the spice and coriander scent of his cologne addictive. It had always been a comfort, but with the way our bodies pressed together, me holding his arms over his head—oh, fuck.

The lust roaring through me was enough to make my head spin.

My erection was undeniable, and I didn't dare look to see what state he was in. When I glanced down at Liam's eyes, the bright blue was almost swallowed up by the black of his pupils. I licked my lips. My throat had turned dry as dust, and I didn't miss how Liam stared at me. Which should've been a lot weirder, but nothing with Liam ever felt weird.

Clearly, my cock had decided to take the helm in the wake of this divorce.

The flood of memories from yesterday rushed through me like an arctic shower, and my erection deflated. Whatever tension had spread between us shattered, and I pulled away despite the itch to plaster myself to him. The past year, I'd been lacking physical comfort. Not that Josie had ever been huge on PDA. If I could have someone attached to my body at all hours of the day, I'd be as happy as could be.

"Okay," I said, needing to keep this from getting awkward. "Do you think Maeve is going to kill us if we commandeer the kitchen to make pancakes?"

Liam lifted his brow. "Only if we head out there like this."

I slid off the bed, even though I wanted to hop in and see if my best friend would cuddle with me a little longer. The idea of returning to an empty house from here on out launched panic signals to my system, and maybe that made me a little demanding, but I was going to get even less of the touch I needed than I already did.

I snatched my wrinkled pants from the floor and tugged them on, though part of me wanted to rewind to when I'd been in bed with Liam. My confused cock stiffened again, and I needed it to calm the hell down. The mixed signals weren't good for my overtaxed brain. I fished my phone out of the pocket of my jeans, but there weren't any messages.

Why would there be? The only people I'd told about the divorce had been at the party last night, and Josie hadn't been super communicative with me when we'd been married, so why would she be now?

A hand settled on my shoulder, and I glanced back. Liam had gotten dressed in pajama pants and his "I have no egrets" shirt I'd gotten him last year. We'd started bird-watching a few years ago, which probably made us old or some shit, but I liked walking through nature with him and catching some cool-ass birds in the meantime.

"Hey," Liam said, his voice deep and serious. "You're going to get through this, okay?"

I swallowed hard. Those were the exact words I needed to hear. "You're not planning on jetting off across the country, are you?" I tried to inject a teasing note into my tone, but it came across plain scared. The divorce would be a hard enough adjustment, but Josie had been part of my life forever. The idea she wouldn't even be around? Hell, I couldn't wrap my mind around it.

"Nah," Liam said, his expression earnest, like he always was with me. "I'm not going anywhere."

Fuck, that lobbed relief straight to my sternum. I leaned toward him, his hand still on my shoulder, but I restrained myself because I'd manhandled him enough this morning. I'd barely begun to process my divorce, and I wasn't at the point of picking apart my libido's reaction to Liam this morning.

"Pancakes," I said before my brain wandered again without my permission. "Let's go ransack your kitchen."

"All right." He stepped past me to lead the way to the kitchen.

I followed him, and my gaze zeroed in on the prominent curve of his ass.

My cock throbbed.

Somehow, I didn't think pancakes would make this attraction disappear.

Chapter Three

Liam

I settled into my seat with my large, steaming cappuccino in hand.

Afternoon coffee was beyond necessary after last night and this morning, and Maeve had forced me out of the apartment. This woman, with all her being social and leaving the house needs, would be the death of me. If I perished, she would absolutely be the guilty party.

Though I kind of wanted the breath of fresh air too.

The golden light of the late afternoon sun streamed through the open windows of this cozy spot. Artificer Coffee was such a gorgeous place, with exposed brick walls, dark hardwood floors, a long wooden counter that stretched through the back half of the room, and vaulted ceilings with arched windows. The fireplace in the corner flickered with pretty flames, and folks clustered outside the glass-paned doors to the right, taking advantage of the outside patio.

"Did you see the building across the street is for sale?" Maeve said, plonking down into the seat opposite me. Despite last night being her birthday celebration, she was shockingly not hungover, and her hair was pulled into a ponytail and her wing-tipped eyeliner sharp as a razor.

"And that impacts me how?" I played the avoidance game in full force. I'd been working as a PT for years now, but driving to my job forty-five minutes away had gotten old after the first six months. My dream was to open my own clinic. The clientele was here, I'd saved the funds, and I'd be able to hire some assistants and massage therapists to round out the business. Except every time I sat down to fill out the paperwork, I froze up.

My family, my best friend, and my close-as-fuck friend group were all in the area, and I had no plans to move. I had the experience and the funds. There was no real reason to stall on finding my own place. Yet Hal's words still rang around in my head, on how I was too passive, how I wouldn't be able to handle problems on my own. He'd called me needy, too dependent, and those insults had taken root until I'd made sure I didn't rely on anyone.

Relationships weren't on my radar after the train wreck Hal and I had become, and I refused to lean on friends too much.

However, opening my own business? That involved a lot of trusting in people, depending on people, things I had a hard time doing.

"Right, if you're going to feign ignorance on the prime opportunity for your PT business over there, then I'm going to get nosy about what the hell you and Ollie were doing emerging from your room all rumpled and cute-like."

A fierce flush flooded my cheeks.

"We were drunk and passed out in my room," I muttered, trying my damndest to repress my blush at the reminder of how I'd woken up this morning. Sharing a bed with Ollie hadn't happened since high school, and to blink awake next to all his heat and muscle vaulted me back about fifteen years. However, stripped down to our underwear was a new one for both of us.

Clear by the way Ollie had all but ogled my panties, and when he'd slipped a finger in past the waistband...fuck. Every nerve ending in my body had lit up at the simple touch.

And our wrestling session on the bed would be in my spank bank until I died. His huge frame, those thick muscles, how his thighs had trapped me in—everything had made me want to flip over and offer my ass. However, then he'd pulled back, and we'd made pancakes, avoiding talk about the Josie situation since he'd clearly have to handle it when he headed home.

My phone hadn't made a peep, even though I'd been checking it regularly since he left a few hours ago.

"You're *so* convincing," Maeve drawled, attacking her tea with one of those little wooden stirrers. "As if Ollie isn't the reason you're on the anti-commitment train."

I shot her a glare, a familiar irritation roiling in my chest. "He's not."

I'd tried, and the year with Hal had made me realize that sometimes no relationship was better than that mess. Ollie had nicknamed him "Hell" for a reason. Not like Ollie's marriage had been peaches and cream either. Neither of us had done great in that department, but our friendship was enough for me. Hookups scratched the sexual itch, and I'd had a good routine going.

My phone buzzed, and I glanced at the screen and wrinkled my nose. A text from my boss was the last thing I wanted to see on my day off.

Amanda called out, so we need you to take her patients tomorrow.

Fucking lovely.

"What's got you so pissy?" Maeve asked, nudging my foot with hers.

"Work's doubling my load tomorrow." I groaned. Shit, I'd given her the ammo to pester me.

Maeve's lips curled with her feline grin. "Okay, jokes on loads aside, you know you wouldn't have to deal with this stuff if you opened your own practice, right?"

I shot her a deadpan look. "Yeah, but I'd be dealing with the other headaches, like running a goddamn business."

"You just need an outlet for that pressure," Maeve said, dogged in her determination to see her friends succeed. How dare she want what was best for me. "I bet Ollie's going to be so lonely and horny now that he's single."

My whole body ran hot. Sure, it had been every wet dream as a teenager, and I'd spent an ungodly amount of time jerking off to thoughts of him, but I kept that shit on lockdown. Though Maeve had figured me out a while back, and though Theo was gentler in his approach, I knew he had too.

"All that means is I have to sit through my best friend going through a string of hookups with random women," I admitted the truth, if only to stop my foolish heart from getting invested. Pointless longing was one thing—I'd known Ollie was off-limits for a long time now—but this divorce was dangerous. It cracked open the tendril of hope I'd never fully strangled.

"If Ollie's straight, I'll eat my corset." Maeve took a swig of her tea.

"Which one?" I arched a brow as I tried to ignore the way her definitive statements fed that sickening hope.

"The leather one I bought at Faire last year," she said, giving me a dead-ass look like she thought I was an idiot. And fair. Self-deception didn't work for long around my bulldozer friend.

"Well, I hope you like the taste of boiled leather." I clutched tight to my cappuccino. "I heard it makes a great soup."

An adorable chick walked by with a bright pink bob, crimson lips, and the sort of rockabilly style Maeve lost her mind over.

"Cute-as-hell skirt," Maeve said to the woman, her voice going all throaty in the way it did when she was picking up. I held back my eye roll, barely. At least I kept my one-night stands private.

"Thanks," the woman said, a blush staining her cheeks as she passed us to the counter to order. Maeve kept her gaze plastered on her whole time. If they were hot, femme, and single, Maeve would swoop in with a flirty line. We both kept our shit nondramatic, which was how we preferred it.

Relationships just invited complications.

I'd almost lost myself to one once and would never return to being that guy again.

"Why don't you go get her number." I gestured to the woman. "She's right in line."

Maeve let out a low hum. "And abandon you in your time of need, Liam Dorothy Kelly?"

"That's not my middle name," I grumbled, slugging back more of my cappuccino to savor the robust coffee with the sweet foam. "And I'm not in need."

"That's where you're wrong," Maeve wagged a finger in full lecture mode. "You've always needed Ollie's cock, but now it's unattached."

I cringed. "Please don't talk about separating his cock from his body."

"Some of the best cocks are the detachable ones," Maeve said with a sniff. "And stop being an ass. It's not like I'm running around with a penis guillotine."

I shifted in my seat to move an inch away from her, the chair squeaking with the motion. "Well, now I'm nervous about sharing an apartment with you. I've never even heard of a penis guillotine before."

Maeve reached across the table and flicked me in the arm. "Stop being such a drama queen. What sort of yoga instructor would I be if I moonlit as a castrator to the masses? It'd mess up the energy I'm putting out."

"What, orgy vibes?"

"You're such a little bitch." She huffed and took another sip of her tea. "Like I haven't seen the parade of men who tromp through your door. Just because you keep it on the DL and don't talk about them doesn't mean you're not just as much of a slut."

I snorted, letting the tangle of confusion from last night and this morning drift away. Even though Maeve kept trying to make me confront my problems, and maybe she had a fair point, right now, I just wanted to sit back with my cappuccino and enjoy the Sunday afternoon.

"Hey, cutie," Maeve said as Pink Hair strolled by again, this time walking a bit slower with more of a swing in her hip. Well, this outing would break up soon.

My phone buzzed again, pulling my attention away from Maeve's steady stream of flirting. Ollie had messaged me, and I hated the way my heart always sped the slightest bit at the sight of his name on my screen.

Help! Emergency at the Brannon household!

I sucked in a breath. My drama queen best friend wouldn't text over a true emergency, which meant he was in freak-out mode about the divorce.

I'd been over Mr. and Mrs. Brannon's house to hang with Ollie for as long as I could remember, apart from the brief stint when I'd gone away for college. But the second I came back, they welcomed me back into their loud, chaotic family, since I was not only their son's best friend but apparently "one of them" if Rory's incessant chanting was any indicator. Hell, my family got invites over to their house on holidays. My folks hated the stress of hosting but loved the big, cozy atmosphere over there.

Another text from Ollie buzzed through.

Come save me.

I heaved a sigh and swallowed the last gulps of my cappuccino. Maeve was deep in conversation with Pink Hair, and this would give them the perfect opportunity.

"Hey, Maeve?" I said. "I've got to get going. I'm getting dragged into divorce drama with the Brannons."

Maeve shook her head, a smirk on her lips. "Just make sure to bend over a lot in front of him. Find reasons to stretch."

I flipped her the middle finger as I got up and gestured to Pink Hair if she wanted to take my seat. She slipped into it, and I brought my mug to the designated receptacle before heading for the door.

I would only drop everything for one person on the planet, and his name was Oliver Brannon.

Chapter Four

Ollie

Going to Sunday dinner at my parents' tonight had been poor planning on my part.

I squeezed the steering wheel, willing myself to get out of my Jeep.

My folks had a cape-style house they'd bought when they first got married and raised me and my four siblings in it. We had always had to share bedrooms, at least until Declan headed off to college, and they added a bedroom to the basement. The place was the epitome of chaos, but it was home in a way mine had never felt like. Maybe that should've been a sign Josie and I were doomed to failure, but I'd been so focused on the family business the past six years and before that switching from general contracting to getting my welding certifications.

Josie had been reaching for the stars too, just in a totally different direction.

I leaned back and stared at the roof of the car. I'd sent a desperate text to Liam because the idea of facing my family alone right now with the knowledge of what loomed overhead had my stomach twisting. My family would have questions and want answers I sure as hell didn't have. When I'd swung home, Josie hadn't been there, but her drawers had been open, half of her clothes missing. Chances were she'd already swept through the house and gathered her belongings to leave. Ever the efficient one she was.

I swallowed the lump in my throat, which sat like acid in my gut. Right. Time to go face the horde of Brannons waiting for me. I cracked my door open, the summer air sweeter in the early evening. Based on the other cars in the driveway, we had a full house tonight, which wasn't bolstering my mood.

Maybe Rory would have a weird new piercing for everyone to focus on.

I cut the distance between me and my folks' cute little cape with the cranberry shutters and the matching door all too fast. I walked the familiar stone pathway, avoiding the third stone, which still needed repairing, and the crack down the middle of one closer to the door. The sheer volume from my family quaked from inside. Warmth stirred in my chest, battling with the nausea that had taken root there.

The nausea won.

The moment I pulled the door open, the scent of roasted ham wafted my way, which meant Dad would've made potatoes as well. My father's recipes were often fought over, but no one prepared the family dishes like he could. Mom tried, but we preferred it when she didn't. The woman had wrangled us while working part time as a medical assistant at Chester County Hospital, but a chef she was not.

"Get your feet off the table, Cormac Brannon," Mom barked from across the room, and my brother reluctantly lifted his steel-toed boots from the coffee table. Cormac was only a year younger than me, and we looked similar—both inheriting a lot of Dad's features with his deep-set eyes, thick brown hair, and square jaw.

"Look, if you didn't want my advice, don't ask for it," Aislin said, raising her hands. My little sister had streaked her light brown hair with blue instead of the familiar purple, and she walked by with a natural grace that had drawn admirers from an early age.

Declan strode behind Aislin, emanating pure seriousness, like always. He wasn't built like Cor and me but was slender instead, more like Rory and Ais, and the thick-rimmed glasses and button-downs he wore always made him appear a bit stuffy. Either that or the holier-than-thou eldest attitude.

"I asked for insight on why my date might have ghosted me, not a pithy commentary on my lack of skills with women."

Aislin shrugged. "Look, I'm saying launching into a lengthy explanation on why Mars could be terraformed might not be the best way to woo someone you just met."

"Well, what the hell was I supposed to talk about? The weather?" His voice took on the snippy tone he got when he grew irritated.

I clapped a hand on his shoulder. "If she can't handle your space talk, she isn't the one, D."

"Is Josie coming?" Aislin asked, glancing past me to the door.

I swallowed hard. Hopefully, none of them noticed the way sweat pricked on my forehead. "Nah, she's busy tonight."

"You try doing a Princess Diana piercing by the light of a flashlight app." Rory called into the other room, even as he walked into this one. "That's skill."

"Don't ask what the piercing is," Cormac said to me from his spot on the worn living room couch. "He's been crowing about that one since he came in."

"Would you rather I talked about Prince Alberts?" Rory said, arching a brow as he stopped close to the couch. Piercings and tattoos covered his body from head to toe, peeking out from under his T-shirt and basketball shorts. He looked like a combination of Mom and Dad, slender like Declan and with Dad's thick hair but Mom's sharp eyes.

"Or none." Cormac shuddered. "I don't know how you're comfortable getting needles shoved into you." Out of all our siblings, Cormac was the only one without any ink or piercings, not even the family tattoo the rest of us got. He and I looked the most alike, but I was a few inches taller, which I'd remind him of until we were dead and buried.

"No talking about genital piercings at dinner," Mom called from the kitchen.

"It's not dinner yet," Aislin shouted back.

"It is now," Dad said as he lumbered into the living room. "Come help set the table."

My father and I had the same build—broad shouldered and big—which served us well with the contracting jobs we did. Dad, Cor, and I each had our specialties, and we'd been expanding the business lately, especially since the old man had started slowing down. We could tell he planned on passing the reins over, which worked for me. I'd need something to throw myself into with my impending divorce.

I swept Dad in a quick hug, which he returned with gusto before stepping past him to head to the kitchen. Mom was already collecting plates and utensils. She'd twisted her long brown hair into a low bun, and her glasses aligned perfectly with her no-nonsense features. She was short and slender like my sister, but where Aislin moved with grace, Mom moved with efficiency.

"Here, take these to the table," Mom said, handing over a stack of plates. She leaned in and gave me a kiss on the forehead. "Good to see you, sweetheart."

"You too." I gripped the plates tight. What I hadn't anticipated was how much the normalcy and affection from my family would hit harder than a sledgehammer in the wake of the way Josie had tossed our thirteen years together out the window, like none of our time together had meant anything.

I placed the plates on the dining room table and slipped my phone out of my pocket. No response from Liam yet. He'd be the perfect distraction right now. My family loved Liam, and he usually pulled me out of bleak moods better than anyone.

Even better than Josie had.

I swallowed hard. Despite my wife pulling the plug on our ages-long relationship, a large emotion loomed in the background I wasn't quite ready to name. The fact that I felt like I submerged after holding my breath for so long was telling enough.

"Does Josie still need me to go over her résumé?" Declan asked me as he put the silverware next to each plate.

The truth hovered on my tongue, along with shards of hurt that she'd roped my brother into helping her go cross-country when she'd never told me she was applying for jobs. We'd both been busy this year. Well, maybe the past few years, but if she would've talked to me, I would've listened.

"Nope, she's good." Hopefully, he didn't scrutinize too hard. Dec was the one sibling who'd most likely miss the cues.

The front door creaked.

"Liam," Aislin squealed. "Ollie didn't tell me you were joining us."

Some taut cord in me relaxed at hearing my best friend's name.

A grin ripped to my lips without hesitation as I pivoted in the direction of the front door.

Rory and Cormac were deep in conversation with Dad, but Aislin had slipped her arm through Liam's and led him deeper into the house.

Liam had changed from the sweats I'd left him in this morning into a crisp pair of jeans and a blue polo that clung to his slender frame. His light blue eyes sparkled as he responded to something Aislin said. His grin came easily, like it always did in this house. My heart thumped a little harder, relief flooding through me so fast I almost staggered.

"Wasn't sure if you were going to make it," I said, slipping a thumb into the pocket of my jeans as I slowed my approach. Pouncing on him might sound like a good idea, but this morning that had gone...unexpectedly.

Liam crooked a brow with the snarky expression I loved. "Yeah, no way I could miss such an...exciting dinner."

I fixed him with a "don't you dare" look.

"What's exciting about tonight?" Aislin asked, glancing between us. "Do you have an announcement, Ollie?"

Before I could open my mouth and lie my face off, Liam stepped in.

"I was thinking about getting a puppy, but I wanted to narrow down between a few choices."

I blinked. Had Liam not told me about such a big decision? We talked about everything. "What puppy?" I said before my brain caught up with my mouth.

Liam shot me a "really" look while my sister dragged him to the kitchen.

Right. He was covering for me. Maybe this was why I'd missed the cues of Josie leaving me.

"Come on, you fuckers, it's dinnertime," I called out to the trio on the couch.

Dad looked up. "Is that any way to talk to your father?"

I snorted. "If I didn't hear half the shit you said while we were at jobs, maybe." Working with my father was the best gig, though. Dad cared about the business and his profession, and it reflected in every aspect of the Brannon Contractors.

"I'm sitting next to Liam," I said to Aislin, who had already snagged a seat beside him. He was my best friend, but the rest of my family had long since adopted him.

"You can have this spot." Liam patted the seat next to him. The rueful grin on his lips offered the balm I needed right now—that and his presence. Just being around him, breathing the same air, calmed me down a little, even amid all the chaos.

"Good," I mumbled and plunked into the weathered seat with the black-and-white-checkered upholstery.

The ham smelled amazing, as did the steaming rolls, green beans, and a huge tray of scalloped potatoes Dad had cooked up. All the dishes had his trademark attention to detail.

Liam held up his phone to show Aislin his imaginary puppies for purchase. He thought on his feet faster than anyone I knew.

"You should get a golden retriever." I pointed at one of the puppy listings he had up.

"Why do that when he already has you?" Aislin shot back, giving me a look.

I looped an arm around Liam's shoulder and dragged him a little closer. "And you're stuck with me too." The statement meant a little more tonight, with everything in my home life so unstable. This close, I got another comforting whiff of Liam, slightly spicy and sweet, and

I couldn't help but wonder if he was wearing the same panties as this morning.

My cock woke up real fast.

I let go of Liam and scooted my chair under the dinner table a bit more.

"I'm just saying if you want a meaningful relationship, maybe Grindr shouldn't be your go-to," Rory said to Cormac as they settled in at the table.

"We can't all be lucky like Ollie and fall for our high school sweethearts." Cormac grabbed a fresh roll from the bowl. Mom leaned over and whacked him in the arm. My stomach dropped at Cor's comment. Clearly, that hadn't worked out well for me. And the idea of apps or throwing myself into the dating pool again sent my mind spinning. I didn't do well by my lonesome.

"Yeah, but there are dating apps you could try, asshole," Rory responded.

"What a kind and loving family we have," Mom muttered. "I just adore the sweet way you talk to each other."

"Or you guys could make the effort and go out once in a while," Aislin said. "I'm still able to meet plenty of people at bars."

"Ugh, going on dates is obnoxious enough." Declan sliced into the piece of ham. He'd already heaped up his plate while everyone else had been yammering. "Why would I want to add more social excursions onto the pile?"

"I'll go with you to the bar, Aislin," I said before thinking about the words that came out of my mouth. Liam knocked his knee against mine, but when he went to retract, I leaned mine back against his, keeping the contact.

She shrugged. "If Josie wants to wingman for me, all the better."

My stomach dropped. God, the divorce would be brutal to break to the family. Josie had been part of the family for so long, and Aislin and Josie had formed a solid friendship. Hell, it would upset Ais when she found out Josie wasn't just ending our marriage but also leaving the East Coast.

Liam's palm settled on my thigh, the warmth comforting in a way I clung to right now.

"Or you could come visit me at work," Rory said. "The amount of numbers I get is ridiculous. I'm happy to share the love."

"Ugh, I don't want your sloppy seconds," Cor muttered.

"Wow, this ham is delicious," Mom said pointedly to Dad, who let out a low snort. They shared an affectionate look that made my heart ache. That. I wanted that. To be able to communicate wordlessly with a partner because I knew them so well. Josie and I might've gotten along some of the time, but we never had the deep connection my folks did.

"All of you can take your judgment and let me keep on keeping on," Cor said. "If my body count gets a little high, then so be it."

"Body count makes you sound like a serial killer," Declan said.

"Pass the green beans, John Wayne Gacy," Liam said, his blue eyes glittering with amusement. I slid my hand over the one he kept on my thigh and squeezed. His shoulders stiffened, but then he relaxed, and I didn't want to move my hand quite yet. The solidness of his presence, the way he anchored me when everything else flipped upside down, meant the world to me.

However, the shiver traveling up my spine when our glances met was new.

Same as the burst of lust coursing through my veins.

Chapter Five

Liam

"Has anyone ever told you that you're needy?" I said to Ollie as I got out of my car. We'd spent a lot of time attached at the hip, but this divorce would elevate it even more.

He'd asked if I wanted to come over and game. Honestly, I'd wanted to veg out at home, but I'd caved when those soft brown eyes had met mine. And the clinginess I'd expected. Ollie had always been that way, and for some reason, he was the one person where it didn't bother me. Being around him didn't leech out the energy from me like it did with everyone else.

Part of me was fucking thrilled to be spending more time with him.

The other part was terrified at what would happen when he fell for a new woman.

"We already knew that." Ollie said, his keys jangling as he pulled them out and loped toward his house. Josie's car was absent from the driveway, but he'd said she hadn't been home all day.

"Come on." Ollie placed his hand on my lower back as he gestured me inside. He had always done things like that, so I tried not to read into it, but the constant possessive PDA had made me swoon from an early age. Even at dinner earlier, the way he'd rested his hand on top of mine and kept it there—fuck. My heart hurt just thinking about it.

Ollie clicked the door shut behind me and ushered me farther into his house. The cozy rancher, a few streets away from his parents, fit his personality to a T. I'd always been jealous of Josie, but I never hated her. She was chill, and we could shoot the shit about the medical industry, even though we worked in different sectors. She was pharma, like Aislin. When I moved back to the area, I'd expected to not see Ollie as much, but I swung over to hang with Ollie, or he came over to see me most nights. I might have seen more of him than Josie did.

Clearly, that strategy hadn't worked for their marriage long-term, though.

I wrinkled my nose as I took in their living room. The faded spaced on the walls indicated where some of Josie's weird art deco paintings had been, and the bookshelves had some sizable gaps.

"Did Josie start moving stuff out?" I asked as irritation flared through me. "Where's she staying?" She'd dropped the bomb on him yesterday and was already pulling shit off the shelves?

"Fuck if I know," Ollie muttered, scrubbing his palms over his face. "Probably her mom's or something."

I shook my head. "How are you this calm right now? She, what, overturned your life yesterday, and she's already making a dent in the house?"

Ollie let out a long, slow exhale as he all but deflated. "I should be freaking out, right? And a part of me is, but..." He chewed on his lip and dropped into the big black sectional but didn't elaborate.

"Come on, Ollie," I said, plunking down next to him. I didn't keep any space between us, knocking my knee against his. I knew how physical he was, something I adored that killed me in the same breath. "If there's anyone you can talk to, it's me."

"Fine." He stared at the floor, resting his elbows on his knees. "Part of me is just...relieved."

"I think that's pretty normal," I murmured, flicking him in the side. "Newsflash, but you guys never got along great, even back in high school."

Ollie's brows drew together. "Why didn't you ever say anything?"

I crossed my arms. "Wasn't my place, man. You chose her, and I was respecting your decision."

Ollie slumped farther forward, looking dejected in a way I couldn't stand. "I'm aware we were never the ideal...like Mom and Dad. But I don't know. I thought if I kept trying, we'd eventually get to a better place."

My best friend, the perpetual optimist. Even though it drove me crazy sometimes, his sunshine attitude was something I loved about him the most.

"Well, you've got a chance to find the ideal person now," I said. The words tasted bitter on my tongue.

Because the truth was, that ideal person would never be me.

"Whatever. I've got plenty of time before contemplating the wilds of dating." Ollie pushed up in his seat. "Let's play Mortal Kombat and blow off steam. I could use the distraction." He cast me a sidelong glance. "Though a game's not nearly as distracting as wondering if you're still wearing those panties from this morning."

My face flushed, a whole-body torrent of flames. Ollie stared at me with an intensity in those brown eyes that was very different from his normal, affectionate looks. This close, his plush lower lip begged for my attention, and his broad shoulders were such a goddamn turn-on. My best friend had no right to be so fucking hot.

"That's my business," I said, trying with all my might for casual while my insides swooned. "And since when did we talk about underwear?"

"Since one of us had underwear worth talking about." Ollie leaned over to his coffee table where he had two controllers sitting there. He flashed me his slightly crooked smile that made my heart skip a beat. He thrust one of the controllers at me. "How about this? I'll earn your answer. Whoever loses each bout loses an article of clothing."

This wasn't real life, was it? The sexy dip in his voice, his gaze focused on me. Hell, this was every daydream I'd entertained for years.

I swallowed, my throat dry. "So, strip Mortal Kombat? Can't say I've ever played that."

But I sure as hell wouldn't pass up the chance to see Ollie stripped down—especially now that he was single.

"You in?" he asked, the cocky tone to his voice offering relief. When he'd shown up last night to announce his divorce, I thought my sunshine best friend would sink deep into depression. However, the last few years, Ollie and Josie had been heading that way, whether he'd realized it or not. The increasing distance between them, the lack of communication, doing more and more without the other involved.

I knew Ollie, and when he got invested, he got attached.

Kind of like he'd always done with me.

"Guess you better prepare to strip down," I responded, hoping Ollie hadn't noticed how my cock was growing harder. I'd switched my purple panties to a pink satin pair, and the idea of Ollie scanning me down like he had this morning—fuck, my erection already tested the fabric.

"Right, like you're that great at Mortal Kombat." He settled into place, his knee nudged against mine, our legs touching like they usually did. Except now I was more than aware he wanted to see what I wore beneath my clothes, and my hopeless heart didn't know what to do with that information. My cock was one thousand percent on board, though.

The familiar opening screen kicked on, and we chose our fighters, each of us sticking with comfortable territory. I picked Mileena, while Ollie went with Sub-Zero. He was better at this game than me, and to be honest, the thought of that thrilled me a little. Indulging in any of this wasn't healthy, especially not the day after Josie had told him she was leaving, but I'd been yearning so long for him to even look with the slightest flash of something…more.

I just wanted his eyes on me a little longer.

Before he threw himself back into the dating pool. Before he found the love of his life and married some new woman who'd steal him away.

"Round one…Fight!" came from the screen, and I snapped my attention to the game. We both launched into the bout, the tap-tap-tap of button-mashing fast and furious. Ollie might've refined a technique, but I tended to spam the same moves over and over again until I got lucky. He usually won when we played, and we both knew it. Despite the familiarity of our normal rhythm with this game, tension percolated through the air, awareness prickling across my skin.

I launched in with Mileena, a flurry of kicks and hits, but within moments, Sub-Zero was wiping the floor with her.

"Feeling cocky now?" Ollie asked as we waited for the next round to cue up.

I licked my lips, which were suddenly too dry, and I didn't miss Ollie's gaze zeroing in on the motion. Fuck.

"Round Two...Fight," announced the speaker, dragging me back into the match. I'd played with a hard-on before, and I would play with a hard-on again.

If anything, I lost even faster this time.

Ollie crossed his arms and stared me down.

I lifted a brow, fixing him with a look as I removed my sneaker and took off a sock. "If you thought I was starting with anything else, you were sorely mistaken."

"Fine, be like that," he teased as he gripped the controller. "This is only the first bout."

I settled in, down one sock, and Ollie started the next round. Wearing a single sock felt weird, but it made me more aware of the end goal. Which was Ollie getting me out of my pants.

If only that meant what I wished it did.

What had started his obsession with my panties was beyond me, but I wouldn't pass up the chance to have this big bear of a man fixated on me.

The next match passed in a blur, and Ollie focused like hell on the win, which just got me hotter. I ditched my other sock. I'd been barefooted in Ollie's house plenty of times, but the intent behind it had my skin prickling and my heart thumping harder.

"It's like you want to strip down for me," Ollie murmured. "Get prepared to lose more—in both regards." His dark eyes were dancing, and his lips curled up in a mischievous grin. It was hard to believe this was the same guy who'd been all rain clouds last night.

I chewed on my lower lip as I wiped out at yet another round of Mortal Kombat. Truth be told, I loved having Ollie's eyes on me like this, and I knew the more skin I showed, the more he would be looking. He'd always been physically affectionate, but the slight darkening of his gaze, his heady focus turned my way? Never.

The screen flashed my loss, and I sucked in a sharp breath as Ollie set down his remote on the end table and propped his arms against the back of the sectional.

"Your choice," Ollie said, the confidence radiating off him. I swallowed hard, trying to ignore how my cock woke the fuck up at those low words. The huskiness in his voice, the heat blazing in his gaze was nothing I'd ever expected to be leveled my way, and I still questioned this freak anomaly in our friendship.

However, I was here for the ride.

I pursed my lips and grabbed the hem of my polo, which wasn't the sexiest thing I could've worn, but I'd work this as best I could. Trying to shut out that Ollie—my Ollie—was the one watching me, I lifted the shirt up my waist the way I would if I was getting flirty with a hookup. Just a slow glide of fabric along my already sensitized skin from the sheer magnetism of Ollie's gaze on me. My mind spun, and this close, I got a lungful of his scent, all metal and patchouli.

My cock was at full-mast now, but I ignored how my jeans strangled my erection as I brought the hem up higher, flashing a nipple, then sneaking it back down.

"Tease," Ollie said, his voice hoarse and warm. Lust coursed through me like a sip of whisky.

My lips quirked in amusement. Even when I vibrated with this cocktail of adrenaline, somehow Ollie made this easy, natural. He'd seen me shirtless a thousand and one times before, but it had never felt like this. Then, it had been a circumstance, but in this moment, I was stripping down solely for him. I flicked a few buttons of the polo open, soaking in the way his gaze glued to my chest, how his breathing came in a little heavier, how his pupils were blown out.

I finally slid the hem of my shirt up and over and tossed the shirt onto the ground.

"Well, damn." Ollie let out a low whistle. "Why haven't we been playing strip Mortal Kombat sooner?"

Ollie's shoulders froze, and I knew the realization of why snuck in, threatening to shatter the tension between us. However, I didn't want this moment to end, for him to draw his gaze away from me.

"Well, you're single now." Yeah, I was playing with fire.

"Oh?" Ollie said, his gaze sliding from my chest to my eyes, and a shiver rolled through me at the intensity in his gaze. "So, what other games have I been missing out on?"

His intent was crystal clear, and oh, holy hell, I was burning up from the inside out.

I opened my mouth, not sure how to respond with how my entire body reacted to Ollie's attention. I'd yearned for these sorts of looks from him for so damn long that I couldn't even process my reality. However, the fact we were sitting so close didn't escape me, my knee still brushed against his thigh. The music for Mortal Kombat's loading screen blared in the background, but it was drowned out by the roar in my ears as neither of us looked away.

Ollie licked his lips, which made his lower glossy. My breath hitched in my throat, and the steady *thump, thump, thump* of my heart grew in volume with every passing second.

"I can think of one," he said, his voice all sex and gravel.

I'd seen my best friend every which way over the years from top-of-the-world exhilarated when he did parkour to the infrequent moments when his sunshine faded and the rain clouds rolled in, but I'd never witnessed him like this. Imagined it, yes, a thousand times, but the heat banked in his gaze and the lust dripping from his tone—fuck, it was plucked out of so many wayward daydreams, and the gravitational pull between us was unstoppable.

He began to lean in and close the distance between us. My heart threatened to leap out of my chest as the thrill of this moment roared inside me.

The front door opened with a loud bang.

"Ollie, are you home?" Josie's voice shattered the tension between us like a baseball through glass.

Ollie sat straight as if his spine was an iron rod, and panic flooded through my veins. Shit, I was sitting here without a shirt on.

We'd been about to kiss a mere day after Josie announced she wanted a divorce.

Fuck, what kind of friend was I? Hell, what if Josie had shown up to tell Ollie she'd changed her mind? I swallowed bile as I leaned down and swiped my shirt from the floor.

"In here," Ollie called, his throat a little hoarse and unsteady. He wasn't pushing me away, but he wasn't looking my way either, and if he told me to get out or that this was a mistake, I'd pretty much die on the spot. I grabbed my own life jacket.

"I've got to go." I slipped on my socks and shoes in a record time as all the heat, the comfort, and the thrill withered away like magnolia petals at the first frost. My throat tightened, and I couldn't say anything more to Ollie. I didn't even bother patting down for my keys before bolting for the door.

Josie was dressed in a white tee and jeans, her blonde hair pulled into a low bun. She looked tired, but who wouldn't, given her situation? "Hey, Liam," she said, but I didn't stop to chat. What if she could see right through the shame burning my cheeks?

"See you, Josie." I tried not to be a complete jackass, despite the way my mouth didn't want to work right now. I burst out the door into a night threaded with the kiss of rhododendron and freshly mowed lawns that had mere hours ago smelled like a summertime promise.

Now the shadows twined around my limbs, making every step toward my car drag.

I'd let those hopeless longings get the best of me, but Josie's arrival had delivered the splash of ice water I needed.

No matter how much I wished it were so, Ollie would never be mine.

Chapter Six

Ollie

My heart still hadn't calmed down from—well, all of it. Leaning in and wanting to kiss my best friend, my soon-to-be ex-wife walking into the house, and said best friend bolting out the door. Yeah, so maybe I had a bit to process.

Too bad I wasn't ready.

Josie walked into the living room, casting a glance to the door that had slammed shut after Liam rushed out. "I'm guessing he hates me now, right?"

I ran my fingers along my beard and tugged at the middle. Josie had been the furthest thing on my mind tonight, and that should make me feel a hell of a lot guiltier. But despite the initial punch to the gut, we weren't shedding any tears for a reason. What Liam said had been the truth. Josie and I had never gotten along great, and the past few years had been like having a roommate I occasionally fought with.

"Nah, he just realized what time it was," I said lamely, the excuse sounding shit to my ears.

Josie didn't give me a hug like she would've a few days ago or lay an absent peck on my lips, and the shift made my chest throb. Instead, she plunked onto the sectional, keeping some space between us. The casual affection in the past had been nice, even if it hadn't been the wildfire I'd always dreamed about.

I swallowed hard. I'd just experienced pure fire—the way my pulse still hadn't calmed down, how my skin had grown sensitized from awareness. Every fiber of my being had been tuned in to Liam Kelly, and that discovery delivered a punch to the solar plexus.

Who could have known my best friend would be a powder keg of heat and promise?

"You don't need to lie to make me feel better," Josie said, picking at her nails since she wouldn't look up at me. "I know your family's going to be pissed at me too."

I shrugged. "If they are, they are, but I'm not leading the charge or anything."

"You realized too?" she said, her tone hesitant. The woman I'd lived so long with—thirteen damn years—appeared wholly different for the first time. Sure, she had the same golden blonde hair I'd run my fingers through, the curves I'd gripped when we used to have a healthy sex life. Dark brown eyes that softened in amusement often, and a smirk so razor sharp it could slice. She was damn attractive and knew it, and she was talented as fuck.

However, now that I understood the truth I'd been avoiding—that we'd spent most of our relationship trying to force ourselves into boxes that never felt quite right—I saw she was never really mine.

Just like I'd never really been hers.

"Yeah, Jos," I said, my voice softening. "We've both been stubborn, haven't we?"

She nodded, her eyes shimmering with tears. "I didn't want to hurt you, but we weren't working."

I sucked in a sharp breath, a resolve I'd never expected when she'd broken the news settling in my chest. I pushed up off the couch, sat next to her, and wrapped my arms around her. Josie leaned into me, her shoulders shaking as she sobbed.

"Hey, it's okay." I hugged her tight, part of me not wanting to let go. The truth smacked me in the face with a two-by-four. We'd been sitting in a lukewarm tub together, trying to heat it up with water that had long since run cold. Tears dripped onto my shirt, and I clutched her a little harder, soaking in the time with her before everything changed.

And hell, it was changing at a rapid-fire pace.

"Sorry I already started moving things to my mom's," Josie said as she pulled back. "That probably came as a shock." She wiped at her eyes, the wedding band still on her finger glinting in the light.

I squeezed her shoulder. "Just don't go rushing off to the other side of the country without saying good-bye, okay?"

"I promise."

"Sure, but does that mean a whole lot, given the whole impending divorce?" I teased, trying to lighten the mood.

"You ass," she said, shoving at my shoulder. "You're seriously joking about this now?"

I grinned. "Come on, it's me. Did you expect anything else?"

She shook her head, even as her eyes crinkled. "I'd expected you to hate me, so I'll take your teasing any day."

Maybe it was insane to be so chill about my divorce, but the fact that I wasn't feeling the host of complicated emotions I should've been told me everything I needed to know. Josie and I weren't meant to be together, and it was high time I found the right person.

A little flutter stirred in my chest, and I stared at my hands.

The flirtation between me and Liam was brand fucking new, but the feeling of desire wasn't. I understood what had flared between us when we'd been gaming on the couch, the tension in the air during our little bout of strip Mortal Kombat.

And if my best friend thought he could dismiss what had happened and escape out my door without me following up, he was sorely mistaken.

The salty scent of the Wawa breakfast sandwiches I'd picked up tempted me. My stomach was empty as hell, but I strode up the walkway to the rental Liam shared with Maeve. The familiar sight filled me with warmth, the white house with the pale gray roof that had been split into apartments. He'd been living there ever since he moved back into the area, and I'd spent many a night at his place, sleepless or otherwise. The sun crested the horizon, a trickle of red and gold permeating the gray of early dawn.

Josie and I had talked the rest of the night and hashed out how we'd divide our belongings up in the divorce. I would buy her out of the house, since I planned on staying in the area, and we had such different tastes that splitting our belongings would be pretty simple. Overall, everything had gone a lot easier than I'd thought it would, and that had filled me with immense relief.

What wasn't okay was the lack of a response to the text I'd sent Liam.

Which meant I needed to bother him before he headed out to work. Sure, we might've traipsed into different territory last night, but Liam Kelly was still my goddamn best friend, which gave me the forever right to show up on his doorstep at all times. I juggled the breakfast sandwiches and coffee with one hand while slipping my key into the door with the other.

When I stepped inside, the lights were on, which wouldn't be Maeve's doing. She was the opposite of a morning person.

"Hey, Liam." I kept my voice low so as not to summon his roommate like goddamn Beetlejuice and closed the door behind me.

Rustling sounded, and a moment later, Liam stepped into view. "Ollie?"

Liam wore plaid pajama pants slung low on his hips so the vee leading down was prominent. Not like I hadn't seen him shirtless a million times, but after the way he'd been teasing me last night, I viewed him in a different light. The light sprinkle of hair across his pecs, the tapered waist. His blond hair was tousled from sleep, the strands drifting across his forehead, and the sleepy look in his eyes reminded me of wrestling around with him yesterday.

My cock woke up, so I zipped past him and walked to the kitchen. I placed the bag of breakfast sandwiches and the two coffees on the counter.

"What the hell are you doing here?" Liam stepped up behind me. The scent of him, all spice and coriander, wrapped around me, and I found the comfort addictive. "It's a work day," he continued, confusion clear in his somewhat cranky tone. "I've got to leave in an hour."

"Obviously." I turned around and leaned against the counter, gesturing to the items I brought. "Hence the Wawa stop."

"Okay," Liam said, rifling his fingers through his hair as he glanced between me and the bag on the counter. "Am I missing something?"

I crossed my arms and stared at him. "You bolted out of my house last night without even a good-bye. And then you didn't answer any of my texts."

Liam shifted his gaze away from me as he reached for one of the coffees in the tray.

"This one's yours," I said, plucking the other out. "Irish cream."

Liam's cheeks pinked, and I blinked and then blinked again. Part of me had thought the flirtation was in my head, but no, my best friend was responding to me like he might actually be attracted to me. My heart fluttered. Liam had come out to me back in high school, and I'd never given it a second thought. I always had a string of girlfriends, and then I got steady with Josie, so I hadn't questioned my sexuality.

Guess the lost time was coming to bite me in the ass.

"Josie had shown up, and I didn't want things to be awkward," Liam said as he clutched his coffee tight.

I heaved out a sigh. "Yeah, we had a talk last night."

Liam's throat made an audible click as he swallowed. "How did that go?"

"Really well." I grabbed my coffee as well. The heat from the cup warmed my palms. Liam still wouldn't look at me, which was driving me insane. I might be losing my wife, but I definitely couldn't lose him. I edged beside him until our thighs touched, the contact soothing something taut inside me. "What you said made me think, and Josie and I agreed this divorce was a long time coming."

"Wait." Liam finally lifted his gaze. Those bright blue eyes locked on mine, all serious. "You're not getting back together?"

My forehead wrinkled. "What the hell gave you that impression? Liam, she's moving across the country."

A shaky sigh exploded out of Liam, and he shook his head. "Never change, babe."

"Don't plan on it," I said, opening the bag with breakfast sandwiches and picking out the bacon on a bagel with egg and cheese. From here, the clear view of his window featured a pretty view of a backyard the apartments shared, with a large oak tree and a few smaller crabapple trees. I didn't bring up what I was pretty sure would've been a kiss last night because there wasn't enough time. However, Liam was crazy if he thought we could sweep everything under the rug—because I refused to.

Movement fluttered by the window, and I wandered over with my coffee in one hand and breakfast sandwich in the other.

A bird flitted onto one of the branches of the oak tree, trilling, then calming down.

"What type is it?" Liam asked.

I grinned. "Tufted titmouse."

Liam snorted. "I swear to fuck, that never gets old." A moment later, he stepped beside me, and I basked in his proximity. "Did I tell you about the red-winged blackbird I spotted the other day?"

I arched a brow. "First you're bolting out my door, and now you're not telling me what birds you saw for the day? Are we even friends anymore?"

"I don't need to report my daily activities to you."

My lips pursed in amusement, and I didn't pull my gaze from him, fully conveying where my mind had taken the statement.

Liam's cheeks flushed, and he punched my shoulder. "You know what I mean."

A thrill rose in me I hadn't expected in the slightest but one I clung to now. "Hmm, I don't. With all the secrets you're keeping from me, it feels like I need to up my game."

I waited to see if the comment would land, and the way Liam's pupils flared was a reward in and of itself. He licked his lush lips, and I was mesmerized by the movement. I'd noticed he was attractive before, but I'd been in a relationship forever, so I'd never daydreamed beyond that.

However, now, my imagination seemed to be making up for lost time.

If I crowded him against the window, would I feel his erection pressing against me through the thin fabric of his pajama pants? I glanced down, trying to catch a glimpse of if he was as turned on as I was. I thought I saw the faint outline, but I'd need to be closer to get a better idea. My heart thumped hard, loud enough that it must be echoing through the room.

"Ollie." His voice was throaty and wrecked, so different from how he'd said my name through the years. His blue eyes were big, too damn pretty, and his slight scruff made me wonder what it'd feel like if we kissed.

This felt private in a way that made me shiver, and I couldn't stop the pulse of desire pumping through my veins.

"Why did no one invite me to this prework party?" Maeve's voice broke through the moment. She trudged into the room from the hallway, her flame-red hair tied back in a sloppy bun, squinting at me like I was a hallucination.

I gripped my coffee a little tighter, and Liam tore his gaze from me as if we hadn't just been eye-fucking each other in the middle of his apartment.

Which was undeniable at this point.

Neither of us had brought up the attraction that had flared between us, and I might be dense sometimes, but a five-alarm heat had emerged, and I couldn't resist the draw. It was like stepping outdoors on the first spring day of the year, listening to the birds tweet, and seeing the sun sparkle on fresh buds. I'd been in hibernation with Josie for so long that this explosion of life that burst around Liam had me ensnared.

"Ollie brought me breakfast," Liam said and stepped away from me. Maeve let out a grunt, and a second later, mugs clattered.

My heartbeat still hadn't slowed as I watched the flex of Liam's ass in those pajama pants. He might've dove onto the escape that Maeve had offered, but I wasn't ready to drop this.

Next time, we wouldn't have interruptions.

Chapter Seven

Liam

Trivia night was something I rarely participated in but often attended. Mostly because watching Maeve and Rhys get rabid about winning entertained me, but tonight, I swung by as a survival mechanism.

The past week, when I wasn't working, Ollie got up in my space, whether it was catching me for dinner, taking a bird-watching walk, or swinging by with breakfast. Maeve had joked that my boyfriend might as well move in at this point.

The worst part about all this was that I fucking loved it.

I adored the nonstop time with Ollie, the closeness, the way our bodies kept finding excuses to brush against one another, to touch, to be near. Which meant I'd been in a perpetual state of turned on. I'd jerked off so much this week that I was pretty sure my dick would fall off.

I leaned back in the booth seat at Fun-Guy Sports Bar, nursing a pint of lager while Maeve and Rhys bickered over inane information on the Victorian era, which was this month's topic for trivia night. Cole lost himself in a discussion with Theo and Lex about one of his earlier plumbing jobs, and I just enjoyed not having to talk for the first time all day.

"Who was the dead kitten tea party guy?" Rhys asked, tapping his fingers on the tabletop.

"Ew, what?" Theo asked.

"Walter Potter," Maeve burst in, a live bomb of enthusiasm. "The taxidermist."

I shook my head, casting a glance to Cole. "You're the one dating him."

Cole's grin spread across his face, all dreaminess. "Yeah, I am."

"Better brush up on your Victorian-era knowledge, gorgeous." Lex nudged Theo in the side. "If you fuck up, I'm pretty sure one of these guys is going to shank you."

"He understands the stakes," Rhys said darkly as he skimmed his phone for god knew what other Victorian trivia tidbits he could find.

"Who's your fourth?" I asked. Theo, Rhys, and Maeve were the staples, and they dragged someone else into the fray every month.

"Remember the chick from the coffee shop?" Maeve waggled her eyebrows. Of course I remembered her. I ran into her in our kitchen in the morning, midweek. "She goes to steampunk conventions and is a huge Victorian buff, so we invited her to this one."

I placed a hand on my chest. "You're seeing her beyond a single night? Better start picking a wedding date."

"You're one to talk, Liam Kelly," Maeve said. "Don't think I'm unaware of how often a certain Brannon boy is over our apartment."

"What, Cormac? I'll tell him to go get a life," I said, my skin prickling at the indirect mention of Ollie.

Theo wrinkled his nose. "I thought Ollie was straight."

"Please." Lex draped an arm around Theo's shoulders. "That boy has bisexual written all over him."

My heart tumbled at hearing someone else say the secret wish I'd been clutching tight for too many years. And with the way Ollie kept looking at me like he wanted to kiss me—how I'd been almost positive we were going to multiple times now—my terrible, hopeful heart believed that might be true.

Perfect recipe for heartbreak.

"Speak of the devil." Cole gestured toward the door. "You didn't tell me he was joining us tonight."

I blinked twice. Ollie strode in, still in his jumpsuit with the Brannon name stitched on, the sleeves rolled to his elbows, looking like pure, rugged sex. My fingers itched to run through his thick, windswept hair, and when his brilliant smile burst on his face and his eyes lit up, my heart beat faster.

"Definitely bi," Rhys said.

I balled up a napkin and lobbed it Rhys's way. "Shut up. He's coming over here."

"Hope you don't mind me joining tonight." Ollie walked right up to our booth. "Liam said you guys usually do trivia night, and I've got all this spare time on my hands right now."

Cole scratched his nape as he looked up at Ollie. "How are you faring with that?"

"I think my house might be haunted," Ollie said, scrunching his nose. "There are a lot more thumps than I realized at night."

I swallowed hard, wanting to hurl myself at Ollie. He hated being alone. Not like he needed someone chatting all the time, but after coming from such a big family, he was used to having other people around him.

"He meant about the divorce," Maeve said, blunt as always.

Ollie shrugged. "Josie and I weren't right for each other. We just sucked at acknowledging it."

Lex leaned in and whispered, "Bet there's something else he'd like to suck."

I elbowed him right between the ribs, gratified by the curse he let out.

"You're always welcome to hang with us," Theo said, smoothing over everyone else's obnoxiousness. I wanted to hug him for that alone.

"Come on." I patted the small open space beside me on the booth. Because I clearly could survive being squished up against his massiveness. Fuuuuck. The thought of his body crushing me into the mattress had saliva pooling in my mouth. Hell, I'd love to live between his legs.

I picked up the silverware and sucked on the spoon, needing something to stave off the need rushing through me right now. No one questioned it. They'd known me long enough. Whenever I got anxious, ends of pens, spoons, straws, anything I could suck on for a little while usually made its way into my mouth. So sue me. I had an oral fixation.

Ollie slid in beside me, the tang of metal and sweat emanating from him, which always hot-wired my brain to think of sex. He'd been welding all day, and those scents lingered on his skin, which made me want to get down on my knees for him that much more. The gauges in his ears, the little nick at his chin from an old scar, all of it just turned me on even more. Tonight was supposed to be a distraction from the insane attraction I had for my best friend, but the crush I'd kept a handle on for over a decade now amplified a thousandfold.

I sucked on the spoon a little harder, trying not to pop an erection while I squished in a booth beside Rhys and Ollie. Rhys all but climbed into Cole's lap, as much as he could. These booths were long enough to fit six people, but we were full-grown adults and now at seven. Ollie didn't bother making space between us. He simply wrapped his arm around my shoulders and tucked me into his side.

My heart fluttered. This man did everything I could want—from the excessive PDA that worked so much better than words to the way he constantly took care of me. My attempts at relationships had paled in comparison to the connection Ollie and I had, so why even try for much beyond sex? Especially after the disaster of Hal.

"Cute." Ollie leaned in and tugged at the end of the spoon in my mouth. His eyes glittered with playfulness, and the drool almost dripped from me at how effortlessly sexy those smooth, teasing gestures were. He touched me with a possessive ease that stroked something deep inside me. Like I was whole and perfect and not flawed and chipped from my tumbles throughout the years.

"Where's your lady friend, Maeve?" Rhys said, his leg jostling against mine as he tapped his foot on the floor. "If Candace shows up late, we're going to have to drag one of these fuckers in. And I doubt any of them know shit about the Victorian era."

"Hey, I'm offended," Lex said. "I might be half-rats, but I'm here to take the egg any day of the week."

"Don't mind him," Theo said. "We've been watching a lot of Ripper Street."

"Candace texted she was on her way," Maeve said. "She'll come."

"Bet that was what you said last time," I mumbled around the spoon in my mouth. I removed it and placed it on the table. Ollie's gaze burned into me, and when I glanced at him, he didn't look away. Instead, he just stared at me, heat blooming in his expression. My skin felt stretched too tight, and sweat pricked on my forehead, probably from being tucked against this furnace of a man.

"Fuck, I want someone to make me come," Ollie said to Maeve, and my cheeks burst into flames. She sent me an arch look full of "why don't you do it." I shifted in my seat, my cock going stiff as hell at the idea of an orgasm with Ollie.

"Been a while?" Rhys asked, his expression sympathetic.

"Fucking ages," Ollie groaned, and with the way I was curled up against him, I felt the rumble of his chest. "If I needed any clue that my relationship with Josie was dead in the water, that was one of about a dozen signs."

"You mean the constant fighting wasn't a tip-off?" I asked innocently, trying to distract myself from the raging lust burning me from the inside out.

Ollie squeezed his arm around my shoulders tighter. "You've met my family. Of course that wasn't a tip-off."

I snorted. "Fair." The Brannon household was a detonated bomb of bickering every time the family gathered together, which was often.

The door to the bar swung open, and Maeve's pink-haired damsel entered.

"Told you," she said with a smirk.

I rolled my eyes. "Like you haven't been stood up before."

"Who would stand up all this?" she said, gesturing from her artful red waves to the boho ensemble of an olive green crop top and drapey earth-brown skirt she wore.

"What are you drinking?" Ollie helped himself to my beer. His pink tongue darted out, and the beer glossed his lips after he put the glass back down. Fuck. I wouldn't be able to handle this tonight. I needed to get home to jerk one out or something before my cock exploded and I embarrassed myself. Ollie hadn't picked up that his presence was driving me insane, and I couldn't do a damn thing about it.

Those daydreams of him finding the nearest surface, bending me over, and fucking me until I sobbed were the culmination of years of pent-up longing. However, if I didn't get out of this bar soon, I was going to say or do something I regretted.

"Why don't you finish it?" I said, nudging the glass toward him. "I was just swinging out for a little bit before their match started. I'm going to head out."

Maeve's brows drew together. "Are you sure you want to walk back? I drove us."

"I'll bring you home," Ollie said. His pure goddamn sweetness made me want to scream. "But I'll take you up on finishing your beer. It's been a fucking day." He brought the glass up to his lips again and tipped back. His Adam's apple bobbed as he chugged, and I had to swallow the sigh threatening to escape my lips. When I glanced across the table to Lex, he made a blow job gesture with his hand and mouth while waggling his brows. I was going to murder him. Theo smacked Lex in the arm, and Ollie placed the pint on the table.

"Thanks," I said, not putting my foot down like I should have. Maybe if I pretended I was sick, I could get him to leave me off at the door. Anything but the delicious agony of having him in my bed again. Waking up next to him, those broad arms wrapped around me. It hurt too damn much, and my dick couldn't get enough relief from my hand.

"Have fun tonight," Rhys called out, a twinkle in his eyes. I wanted to strangle him too. My friends were all assholes.

"Thanks, guys," Ollie said, pure sweetness. "I'll stay longer next time, I promise." He pushed out of the seat in a smooth motion, and he hadn't taken more than a few steps forward before turning to look at me. "You coming?"

Someone snorted behind me, but I got out of the booth and followed him, not giving my dickbag friends the satisfaction of looking back. The chick Maeve had fucked passed us, and I offered her a nod. I doubted I'd see her again.

The summer night air was heavy and warm, doing little to offer me relief as Ollie and I walked to his truck. A few folks hung around outside the building, the glow of their cigarettes stark against the shadows and the murmur of their conversations drifting my way. When I settled into Ollie's truck, the tension that had been buzzing through me ratcheted higher.

"Are you okay?" Ollie asked. "I didn't want to ask in front of everyone else, but you seemed off tonight."

My heart cracked wide open. This man was fucking terrible for my self-preservation because of the sweet way he cared, how he put me first over and over again. "Just a stressful day. You know how it can be."

"You need to start your own practice," he said as he started the engine, the rumble vibrating beneath my feet. Within seconds, we hit the road, except he wasn't heading toward my apartment.

"Where are you driving to?" I scanned the road, which led south, right out of town.

"Trust me," he said, flashing a gorgeous grin that lit up those soft brown eyes. Fuck. My pulse thumped so hard it was a miracle he didn't hear it. The truth was, I did trust him, more than anyone on this earth. Except he didn't understand just how much of my heart he'd stolen at an early age and how easily he could obliterate it.

After a minute or two, the path he took became clear, and warmth spread through my insides.

"Parrish Trail?" I asked.

"You know it." He slowed the car as he neared the shitty little trail we used to escape to in high school to sit by the bridge and talk. It was closer to our houses than Anson B. Nixon and a lot less crowded, especially at night. We hadn't been there for a while, but when either of us had a shit day, we'd meet here and sneak a beer or sit there and bask in the sounds of nature around us.

My heart felt like it might escape my chest. He didn't understand how this hope poisoned me at a deadly pace now that he was single, now that all my fantasies were brimming again like I hadn't stamped them down for years. He pulled into the parking lot and shut the engine off. His door creaked open, and he hopped out before I could pull my composure together, so I scrubbed my face with my palms and followed suit.

Away from the middle of town, the starry sky grew brighter, sparkling like shards of glass sprayed across a velvet canvas—sharp and beautiful in the same breath. Despite the need and choking longing that had become an Ouroboros inside me, my shoulders gave up their grip, and I breathed in a deep lungful of the sweetened night air, heady with the lazy scents of summer.

Ollie had already made it to the beginning of the trail, but he waited for me by the sign, the trees leaning in and casting his massive frame in shadow. Even in the pitch of night though, my best friend was pure sunlight. His expression lay wide open as he stared at me, and the intensity of all his focus my way made my mind spin.

When I reached his side, my legs were a little shaky, and I wasn't sure how much of a walk I had in me. However, being in this place with him in this moment imprinted in my mind. Like this snapshot in time was one I would need to remember. I sucked in a breath of the thick air, laden with tension and the scent of azaleas, and came to a stop in front of Ollie.

"You're still buzzing." Ollie placed his hand on my shoulder. I shivered, the weight of his palm on me something I wanted to memorize. I looked up at him, but I couldn't spin a lie fast enough to sound believable.

His gaze zeroed in on my lips again, and the telltale tension amplified a thousandfold.

"Can I?" he whispered, his dark eyes blazing. The incredulous tone in his voice was my undoing.

I wasn't sure what he even asked me, but when it came to Ollie, the answer was a thousand times yes. I trusted him more than anyone else on the planet.

He slid his hand up my neck and cupped the back of it, and I barely caught the movement forward.

All of a sudden, his lips were on mine.

When I was a kid, I used to watch the summer storm clouds.

When those darkening swells rolled in, when the tense air crept through and the breeze picked up, I would leap outside and stand there waiting for the first drops to fall. The tiny bursts of water would splash on my skin as my whole body vibrated with the anticipation of the onslaught. And then the sheets of water descended as they swept me away with a giddy abandon I'd never felt anywhere else.

Until this kiss.

My entire body lit up at the press of his mouth to mine, sheer electricity rolling through me. His grip tightened on my nape with a possessive hold I'd never dared to imagine I'd feel in reality—not with him kissing me like he needed this just as badly as I did. The scent of metal, sweat, and the summer breeze surrounded me, and a low, desperate moan escaped me, one he muffled with another claiming kiss.

Ollie tasted like the crisp beer we'd shared, and the heat of his mouth, his big body bracketing mine, the way he launched into control here like it was the most natural thing in the world—everything ramped up the sheer thrill racing through me. Like I'd captured lightning itself. He reached down with his free hand and grabbed my hip, pinning me in place, and thank fuck because that was all I had to keep me upright. My knees were trembling over a fucking kiss like I was still a teenager.

Except I'd been waiting for this one since then.

Dreaming of the moment Ollie would push through the space between us and claim me in every way possible.

He swept his tongue into my mouth in demanding strokes as he deepened our kiss, throwing his whole attention into it like he did everything. The man had a singular focus, and having that turned my way was a heady experience. The emotion welling inside me grew so intense I couldn't stand it. Like this kiss had the ability to break me apart and remake me all over again. Low noises rumbled from him, and the way he crushed our bodies together, how he took what he wanted with each confident kiss, sent me reeling.

This was more than I'd ever imagined, and I'd spent years and years yearning.

Ollie finally pulled back, and our breaths echoed in the air between us. Yet he didn't release his grip on me. Instead, he tipped his forehead against mine in a gesture so sweet that my eyes hazed over.

"Goddamn," he swore, a wonder in his voice that licked through me like a flame, expunging the memories of anyone else and replacing them with him. Only him.

Ollie had kissed me.

He held me against his body like I was something precious, like he'd gotten just as turned on and blissed out as I had.

Ollie was married. Ollie was straight. Ollie would never look at me like that. The mantras I'd chanted for years shattered after this discovery.

I'd made the mistake of losing myself in relationships before, and I'd done a good job keeping things separate for years. Except there was no separate when it came to Ollie. The intensity of this kiss reached deep into my soul in a way no other guy had. He had the power to completely break me.

Chapter Eight

Ollie

I just kissed my best friend.

My forehead pressed against Liam's. I'd reached a critical temperature with the emotions and sensations flooding through me. This was more than I'd felt in years, and I couldn't remember the last time I'd experienced the intensity of this moment. The way Liam melted against my body, how sweet he tasted, the delicious sound of his moans. My cock was rock hard, and my heart was revving.

I stroked my fingers through his blond strands, relishing the softness against my skin, how his body molded against mine. With my hand on his hip, I brought him flush against me, and the moment his erection pressed against my leg, I lit up inside again. Sure, I'd never made out with another guy, and I definitely hadn't gotten up close and personal like this, but this wasn't any guy.

This was Liam.

He'd always meant more to me than anyone else.

Maybe even Josie if I were riding the Honesty Rails.

"Fuck, you've got me so hard," I said. Liam drew his forehead from mine and looked up at me. His eyes were wide as if he were surprised, the normal light blue of them dark like the surrounding night.

"I've got to be dreaming." Liam stared at me as if he expected me to morph into a werewolf any second now.

I brushed my thumb across his plump lower lip, all spit-slicked and pretty under the moonlight. "Nope, we're both here. Though, my god, why didn't you tell me you could kiss like that?"

Liam shook his head. "It wouldn't have mattered—you were with Josie. And hell, you're straight."

I arched a brow. "I don't think that was very straight of me, Liam Kelly."

He spluttered before whipping his head up to meet my gaze again. "Just like that? What sort of alternate dimension did I step into?"

"A very sexy one," I teased, tracing my thumb across his lower lip. A whimper escaped from him, and a second later he sucked my thumb into his mouth. Pleasure shot straight to my groin at the sweet way he tugged at it, from the heat of his mouth, the softness of his tongue. Liam's mouth felt like goddamn heaven.

"That's not even fair," I said. "You already made me horny, and now you're making it worse."

"Want me to make it better?" Liam let go of my thumb.

"Are you offering what I think you are?" My heart thumped so hard it deafened any other noise. We moved at the speed of light, probably way too fast, and I was pretty sure getting involved right after finding out I was getting a divorce wasn't the smartest move. But I'd never been called a genius, and hell, Liam felt right when nothing else in my life did.

"I'm dead serious," Liam said, his voice earnest in a way that had me reeling.

I cast a quick glance at the parking lot, which was in full view. If anyone pulled up, we'd be fucked, and not in the fun way. "Come here." I laced my fingers through his and tugged us farther along the trail, twigs crunching underfoot. Liam stumbled to follow, but we made quick work of putting some distance so we were out of sight. I found a spot where the trees dipped out a little more, and swung around the trunk, bringing Liam with me.

I didn't hesitate, just dragged him up toward my chest again and claimed his mouth. Fuck, he tasted so sweet, so damn addictive. His lips were soft, and even the scrape of his stubble against mine sent shocks of pleasure through me. Liam's body was different from the women I'd slept with in the past, but I was just as turned on—if not more, like I had an emotional boner.

The way he kissed me, the power in his movements, how he whimpered and moaned when I took control was the hottest thing I'd ever experienced.

"Okay, okay," Liam said, pulling away, his voice a little breathless. "Keep making out with me, and I'm going to come in my pants."

"That sounds like a challenge." I reached for his hips to draw him back in.

"I'd rather come while my mouth's stuffed full of your cock."

Holy hell, this man was nuclear-level hot.

I licked my lips, temporarily speechless, then nodded. "Yes, that." I pulled the zipper down on my coverall, then unbuttoned my pants, well aware of the way Liam's gaze fixated on my movements. His breath came out a little choppier as I pushed down my boxer briefs and pulled out my cock. Pre-cum beaded on the tip, and Liam's eyes flared, the look of hunger in his gaze deadly sexy.

"All right, babe," I said, leaning against the trunk of the tree. "On your knees."

His lashes fluttered as he sank down with a mesmerizing grace. Liam looked thoroughly debauched when all we'd done was kiss. Those lips of his were tantalizing as fuck, and it was too easy to recall the many times he had them wrapped around a pen, a spoon, whatever he could find to suck on. His blond strands were messy across his forehead, and his clothing was rumpled in a way that screamed of sex. And hell, I wanted so much more than a blow job in the woods with this man.

But that could come later.

I stroked the length of my cock. "Come on, baby." I cupped the side of his face. "Let's fill your pretty mouth."

I guided his open mouth toward my cock, but I was wholly unprepared for the moment he engulfed the tip in his warm heat. My knees weakened from the powerful sensation as he drew more of my cock in, the feeling fucking divine. As he took me in all the way with ease, I swore low. The bark of the tree was rough against my back as I leaned harder against it to remain upright.

I'd had plenty of blow jobs before, but nothing compared to how Liam deep throated me on first attempt, like he needed my cock more than his next breath. My chest heaved. I wanted to bask in this, to lose myself in how good he felt, to just move. I threaded my fingers through Liam's blond strands, sure I'd never be able to think of them the same way, and gripped tight as I began to shift my hips, pulling out and sliding back in. Liam's moan vibrated against my cock, and hell, the sight of him, cheeks hollowed out as he sucked, those pink lips straining against my girth—slay me now.

My eyes rolled back in my head as I pushed forward, sinking down his throat, and he gagged a little, saliva dripping from his mouth. His lashes fluttered, those pretty eyes glossed over as he bobbed up and down on my cock. He didn't stop moving as he reached down, and an audible *shink* of a zipper echoed through the stark air. The nighttime sounds faded out around me, and waves of pleasure swept through me with such an intensity I couldn't focus on anything more than fucking my length into Liam's sweet mouth.

Beads of sweat prickled on my forehead, and my balls drew up, threatening release, but I didn't want to let go. The tension built and built, but I needed this. Liam's mouth felt too damn good, and I was addicted to the whimpers he made around my girth, the sloppy sounds as I fucked his face, his enthusiasm as tears rolled down his cheeks,. My grip tightened on his hair as I rode him hard. He was so fucking sexy, and I couldn't believe I'd never realized how hot my best friend was.

How he not only tethered me to the ground but could make me soar to the stars at the same time.

I sagged against the tree, the bark prickling against my back, and my breaths came out choppy. My balls were tightening up, and fuck, the sinful heat of his mouth, his throat squeezing my cock tight, the drool dripping from him, all of it was bringing me closer and closer to the edge. I thrust my hips a little faster, earning myself a gag from Liam, but he didn't retreat.

I could faintly hear a rustling from by his legs, and a moment later he let out a blissed-out moan, his eyes rolling back in his head. Had he just come?

His face surrendered to pleasure did me in. All the tension unleashed, and my release slammed in. The cum burst from my cock, but Liam swallowed it all, only gagging a little, which shouldn't have been as hot as it fucking was. My breaths came out in shattered gasps as Liam's throat bobbed, and he finished swallowing me down. Yet he didn't move away, as if he hadn't gotten enough either. Liam stayed on his knees in the dirt trail, his lips wrapped around my softening cock as he stared up at me with those big blue eyes, luminous in the moonlight.

My heart all but lunged out of my chest, but I didn't pull my cock out of his mouth. Instead, I carded my fingers through his sweaty hair, enamored with this whole new side of a guy I'd known for so long. He continued to lightly suck my flaccid cock, but the way his lashes fluttered, the absolute contentment on his features struck me down.

This, I couldn't walk back from.

Seeing Liam in his panties had been a fascination that lit the match, but kissing him? Watching him lean against my thigh, his nose buried in my groin as he sucked my too-sensitive cock tore something open within me. I'd already cared for him with an intensity that Josie had said wasn't normal, but this searing feeling inside bordered on obsession. It was the combination of late-night laughs we'd shared, empty whisky bottles at the bridge on this trail. It was every knocked knee, every shoulder nudge.

And now it was my fingers running through his hair and shivers coursing through my body like I was the one getting petted. The touch, the closeness so acute I could barely breathe.

The hoot of an owl shattered the quiet, and Liam drew his head back. He released my cock, and a pang of disappointment shuddered through me. To be honest, I'd fucking loved the way he'd kept my dick warmed more than I could say or even understand.

Liam wiped the back of his hand over his mouth, and I glanced down. Cum splattered across the dirt path beneath him from where he'd released. Our eyes locked, the soft vulnerability in his settling in my heart. I reached to help him up. He tugged up his pants, tucked his cock in, and zipped up, and I did the same, reassembling myself.

I wouldn't stand for any awkwardness, though.

Instead of breaking the quiet with words I usually tended to fuck up, I bent at the knee to brace myself and scooped him into my arms. He let out a grunt. Liam wasn't a tiny guy, but he was easy enough for me to carry. Between inheriting the big, burly genes of the Brannon family and doing manual labor my whole life, I didn't even sweat.

"Figured your knees could use a break," I said, riding the high of coming down his throat. Hell, the way he gripped my shoulders while I headed back toward my car, his body crushed against my chest, felt so right.

"What gave you that impression?" Liam asked, his lips quirking. The dry delivery soothed something deep inside me.

"Hmm, maybe because we're not twenty anymore."

The soft earth of the dirt path switched to the asphalt as I walked over the parking lot to my truck. I wanted to rub my face on Liam's neck, where the scent of sweat and sex mingled with his spice and coriander cologne. Instead, I lowered him to the ground, but before he got in, I wrapped my hands around his waist and planted a kiss on his lips.

He let out a low moan that vibrated through me, and I slid my tongue in to deepen the kiss. Liam went boneless in my arms, and the curiosity bubbling inside me was insatiable. I wanted to feel all of him, to experience everything with him at once. Our quick moment in the woods wasn't nearly enough. I savored the taste of him, the heat of his mouth, reveling in how that had felt around my cock. My heart lifted in my chest, buoyant as if it tried to rise to the night sky itself.

I pulled back first and flashed Liam a grin. "Let's head to your place."

He crooked an eyebrow, retaining his dry wit despite his swollen lips and mussed hair. "Is that you inviting yourself over?"

"Excuse me," I said, placing a hand over my chest. "I'm a gentleman. I'm not going to just come down your throat and ditch."

Liam's cheeks grew a pretty red color, and I couldn't help but brush my thumb over the heated skin.

"Goddamn, you're pretty."

His pupils flared, like he might go for a round two, which I wouldn't say no to. Hell, I hadn't even gotten to see if he was wearing panties again. Nerves percolated inside me when Liam didn't say anything.

"I can come over, right?"

"Of course." The softness in his tone reached right inside my chest and settled into my heart. He'd always been my person, and I couldn't imagine that changing.

Maybe diving into kissing him and fucking him right after my divorce hadn't been the best plan. If Liam suddenly decided we couldn't be friends or something massive shifted... no, I couldn't go down that path.

The sweet way he looked at me was more than I could ever have hoped for, and I felt like an idiot for not realizing earlier how special the connection between us was. How fucking thrilling it could be.

"Then let's go." I pressed a kiss to his forehead, walked around to the driver's side of my truck, and turned on the engine, the tang of metal strong in here. Liam sank into the seat beside me, and his presence was a solidness I grasped on to right now. Even after seeing him in an entirely different light, he was still my best friend.

In seconds, we were on the road back toward Liam's apartment. I didn't bother making small talk, instead cranking up the obnoxious 80s music I liked. Liam bobbed his head to it, even though he always said he hated it, preferring his boring-as-sin jazz or swoony acoustic songs. The music pulsed through the speakers, and I threw the euphoria coursing through me into belting out the lyrics. With the windows rolled down, driving along the dark and twisty road and my person at my side, I was limitless—unending.

All too fast, the road to Liam's place came into view, and I turned right and crept down to his, the second on the left. When I pulled in front of his rental along the side of the street, brand-new nerves prickled in my veins. I'd swung over here a thousand times over the years, but tonight, I wasn't sure what lay in wait for me.

And the newness, the unpredictability, thrilled me a little. Whether Liam would have me sleep on the couch or if he'd invite me into his bed. My mouth dried at the thought of wrapping him in my arms and falling asleep curled up by his side. Even better if we were both stripped down like we'd been the morning after the party.

I hopped out of the car, and so did Liam, the slam of the doors shutting echoing through the air.

"I don't know about you, but I'm exhausted," I said. Hopefully, that would direct us toward his bed.

"Coy doesn't suit you, Ollie," Liam said as we walked to the front door. "Yes, we can go crash in my bed."

I held back my fist pump, but the giddiness in my heart was everything I needed. Liam's keys jingled as he unlocked the door. When he looked up, I sucked in a sharp breath.

A world of emotions swirled in Liam's blue eyes—warmth, affection, trepidation, and a few I couldn't quite name yet. The gravity of what we were about to do slammed down on me. I'd been floating on experience, throwing myself into the sensations and the thrill of Liam's attention. My heart burst with color after having been in gray scale for so long.

I'd kissed my best friend, had my cock down his throat, and we were about to curl up in bed together. This could end in total disaster.

Yet when he stepped inside the house and beckoned me in, all I could do was follow.

Chapter Nine

Liam

G oing to bed.

I'd been hoping Ollie meant that as innuendo, but as we walked to my room and he was making no moves to heave me onto the bed and fuck me senseless, it registered that he actually meant it. If anything, this route was worse. A quick screw and I could assume he was exploring curiosities with me, getting whatever he needed out of his system after the divorce.

However, sleeping with him tangled me up in more emotions than I could handle.

My fragile heart couldn't take it, but I also knew if I turned this down now, I'd regret it for the rest of my days. Better to experience a single night with Ollie than spend a lifetime wondering.

I stepped into my bedroom, aware of the bear of a man behind me, his presence so intoxicating I wanted to bask in it. Tonight, I wore a pair of lacy red panties, and the idea of stripping to them sent a shiver down my spine while giving me a semi. Ollie reached past me to flick the lights on, and before we even made it a few paces into the room, he'd already tugged at his shirt to start making himself comfortable.

The door shut behind him, and I gawked as his shirt hit the ground, and he attacked his pants next. I'd always kept my gazes furtive, glances stolen, and even the morning we woke up in bed together half-naked, I'd tried to look away from getting an eyeful because I hadn't wanted to make him uncomfortable, but now I openly stared.

Ollie had always stolen my attention—big, brawny, burly—but shirtless, just *unf*. Fuzz covered his chest, and tattoos threaded up his thick arms and ended around his deltoids. Some I'd been there when he'd gotten them, like the twining tree with his favorite types of birds up one arm. Others he'd done while I was gone, like the raven tattoo on his pecs most of his family had done at Rory's studio, Alchemy Ink.

He undid the button and pulled the zipper down in record time, and unlike in the forest when everything had been happening too fast to process, now I soaked in the sight. Ollie's work pants dropped to the ground, revealing the proud, thick cock I'd had in my mouth and those massive thighs, also heavily furred. Fuck, this guy was so hot naked I couldn't stand it, and the fact that he was hard hadn't escaped my attention.

Would begging be out of the question? I wanted that beast buried in my ass so badly I could scream.

Who knew what tomorrow would bring? Ollie hadn't freaked out about his first experience with a guy, but I'd been there before with straight guys, and a hint of unease hovered in the background as I waited for the other shoe to drop.

Ollie stood completely naked in my room now. Dry didn't begin to describe the state of my throat because I was so damn thirsty.

Ollie swept past me and plunked down into the bed, which meant I should follow him, not just stare at him. I yanked at the back of my T-shirt, pulled it over my head, and tossed it away, not caring where it landed. Next, I brought my hands to the waistband of my pants. Ollie ate me up with his gaze, the hunger in those dark brown eyes setting me on fire.

"Don't tell me you're shy now," Ollie said, and that challenge pushed me over the edge. I shucked my pants off, but before I could strip out of my panties, he let out a low groan. "Keep them," he said, his voice hoarse.

My heart thudded hard as I made my way over to the bed, where Ollie lounged like he owned it, his cock hard as steel. Just like my erection was straining the fabric of my panties. The skimpy pair had seemed like a good idea this morning, but little had I known I'd be modeling them for my best friend tonight.

When I lowered onto the bed next to Ollie, I was careful to leave room as if at any moment the spell would break and Ollie would have a gay freak-out and bolt.

However, before I could settle myself against the pillow, Ollie got all up in my space, wrapping his arms around my waist and dragging my body against his. Fuuuuck. I collided with the warm wall of him, chest hair, heat, and hard muscle.

"You were taking too long." Ollie squeezed my torso tight while we spooned on the bed. My back nestled against his front, his prominent erection nudging my ass. I resisted the urge to buck back and grind against it, even though the need to have him buried inside me rose higher and higher with every passing second.

"Are you planning on smothering me in my sleep?" I muttered, as if I wasn't fucking thrilled by the prospect.

"Excuse me. We just made out and had sex in the woods, so you've got another thing coming if you think I'm not going to cuddle the fuck out of you," Ollie said, brushing an idle kiss along my neck. His movements were so casual, so relaxed, as if he'd been bi his whole life and we'd been together for years.

Not freshly divorced and previously straight.

I didn't want to break this spell by questioning where his head was at, though. Right now, I basked in his attention I'd craved for well over a decade, and if tonight was all I got, I'd soak in every second. The fact that he acted like his same old affectionate self made my chest tight with the countless yearnings I'd clutched to for too many years.

The hazy light of the room wasn't making it easier to settle in to sleep, but I also wasn't tired in the slightest. With the way Ollie cozied up behind me, my entire body sparked like a live wire. He relaxed his hold on me, his hand drifting to my hip. He ran his fingertips along the waistband of my panties, and my cock dripped with pre-cum. A full-body shiver racked through me, one I couldn't hide with how we lay pressed together.

His erection slid between my cheeks, only the lace back of the panties keeping us apart—except I could still feel the velvet heat of him, and it was making me delirious with need. I swallowed hard. Would begging to get fucked be a step too far?

"These are so goddamn sexy," he murmured, sliding his fingers back and forth across the waistband. His cock throbbed against my skin, and I whimpered. There was no way I could sleep tonight. "You like that?" he continued in his gravel and silk tone. He shifted behind me, his erection rubbing against the lace as he moaned. "Sorry." His hot breath puffed against the back of my neck.

"No apologies," I said, reaching down and palming my cock, which threatened to tear through the flimsy satin front. "You could do a hell of a lot more."

He swallowed with an audible click, but I didn't dare to look behind me. Otherwise, I would lose my mind and rub myself against him until he fucked me.

"What do you like?" he asked, sliding a callused finger past the hem of my panties. "Would you want to fuck me? Would you want to get fucked?"

My mouth went dry at those words, and a light laugh escaped me. "In case it wasn't clear, I'm such a cockslut I'd take your dick any day of the week."

"Goddamn." Ollie pressed another kiss along my neck, this one close to the juncture by my ear. "That sounds hot as hell. Want me to bury my cock inside you?"

"Mmph." I was unable to form words with the way my brain exploded with this information. I'd figured blowing him wouldn't be that much of a shock to the system, safer territory, since he was newly bi, but here was Ollie offering to fuck or be fucked.

"Is that a yes?" he asked, mirth in his tone.

"Oh god, yes." I moaned, grinding against his thick cock. The idea of having him sinking deep inside me, of our bodies connecting in a way I'd only ever fantasized about was such a dream. I'd expected some trepidation, considering Ollie had never been with a guy before, but instead, he slipped his fingers past the waistband of my panties and wrapped his palm around my cock.

"Ungh." Pleasure jolted through my body at the simple touch.

"That's sexy as fuck." He licked a stripe up the back of my neck as he ran his hand up and down my erection. I was leaking pre-cum like crazy, delirious with need. Ollie's scent, all metal and sweat and patchouli, blanketed me, and I sucked in a lungful, addicted to his scent.

"Please," I said, not giving a fuck if I sounded desperate. My breath came out choppy as he ground his thick cock against my lace-covered cheeks, and if he didn't get inside me in the next few seconds, I was going to combust.

Ollie pumped my cock lazily and moved his other hand up my chest until he brushed his thumb against my nipple. I choked on a breath as the sinful burst of pleasure radiated through me. I loved having my nipples played with, though not as much as I loved having a cock in my ass or my mouth. Something about it let me turn my brain off, let me completely surrender.

Ollie strummed his thumb back and forth over my nipple with one hand while slowly jacking me off with his other. He played me with a confidence I'd suspected he would have in spades, and it turned out my fantasies of him were just as good as the reality. The sensations overwhelmed me, my mind was spinning out of control, and the pleasure overrode my senses until I was humping against his cock in sheer desperation. My throat tightened at the idea of coming without getting the chance to have him inside me.

"I need your cock, baby," I said. Before I could even think about the term of endearment that had slipped out, Ollie removed his hands and pulled away from me, the loss of all his furnace heat a shock. A second later, he was pushing down my panties to my thighs and sitting upright with a creak.

"Condoms?" he asked. "Lube?"

"They're in the top drawer of my nightstand." I glanced back at him, and I was unprepared for the one-two punch of lust the sight delivered. He pushed up onto his knees, his thick, delicious cock jutting out, and the shadows of the room highlighted the cords of his neck, the dips of his barrel chest covered in fur. His dark eyes were seductive, and I melted under his searing stare. Despite the newness of seeing him regard me with that lust, something comforting existed amid the rising thrill because this was Ollie, my Ollie.

I'd been in love with him for years, and no matter what happened after tonight, I'd continue to be there for him. Because he'd always been my person.

Ollie grabbed the lube and condoms from the drawer and tossed them onto the bed.

"I can prep myself," I said, not sure where Ollie's head was at with everything we were doing tonight.

"Hell no, though we're keeping the panties on. You have no idea how hot you look with them stretched around your thighs. Do you think this is the first time I've had anal before? Hands and knees."

I wrinkled my nose, not wanting to imagine how he'd fucked Josie or his girlfriends before her. I'd always tried to tune out the overshare details from Ollie, mostly because my stomach curdled with jealousy of what I couldn't have.

"I'm negative," I said as I got comfortable on my hands and knees, the mattress creaking with the movement.

"I need to get tested," he said. "Last time I got a full workup was a few years ago, and things were good then, but I'll throw that on the agenda." He settled into place behind me and ran his palm across my ass, the touch sending pure electricity sparking through me. "Is that okay?"

"Just wrap up." A lurid thrill shot through me at imagining his cum dripping out of my hole. Holy hell, I would sell my soul for the chance to be with Ollie bare.

My cock hung heavily between my legs as Ollie took his time running those broad, callused palms across my ass cheeks, as if he was trying to memorize the feel. The elastic of the panties bit into my thighs, but I liked a little sting, feeling contained and trapped this way. The click of the lube bottle made my heart accelerate, and saliva pooled in my mouth at the thought of even just his fingers entering me.

The mattress shifted with Ollie's weight, and he gripped my hip as if to steady me.

"Goddamn," he breathed out. "You have one perfect ass, beautiful."

My throat got tight with the immensity of the moment and the realization of who was prying my cheeks open and ready to enter me with his fingers and cock. The way he talked to me, the affectionate caress to my ass cheek with his free palm—all of it was pure Ollie. Sweet, hot, and completely earnest.

"I need your fingers," I said, thrusting my ass back before I got too damn emotional.

"Fuck yes." Ollie growled as he brushed the tip of his lube-slicked finger against my hole. The moment he started to push in, I bore down, relishing the feel of his thick digit inside me. Between his hand on my hip and the finger he slid deeper in, I was burning up inside with need. By the time he shoved all the way in, I was already riding his finger, needing to feel the glide.

"Holy shit, you're so fucking tight," Ollie said, and my lashes fluttered as I soaked in his words. I had always imagined he'd be a dirty talker, but hearing the stream of babble from his lips was hotter than I could ever have realized. He pulled his finger back and nudged a second one in, opening me up for his cock. With the steady way he worked his fingers in, I was delirious for him in no time. The in-and-out slide felt so damn good, but then he crooked the tips of his fingers deep inside.

Fireworks sparked through me, and a loud moan escaped my lips.

"Ohhh, you like that?" Ollie asked, a glee in his voice I wasn't prepared for. He gripped my hip a little tighter and, with focus and precision, began to mercilessly tag my prostate. My breath caught in my throat from the onslaught of sensations.

"Holy fuck, Ollie," I gasped out. "Slow the hell down."

"Like this?" he said, switching his tempo to unbearably slow. As he dragged back at his agonizing pace and pushed his fingers in, he couldn't resist tapping my prostate again. Those sparks flared through me even harder this time, and I couldn't help the long, slutty moan that escaped me in the process.

I glanced back at him, and the smirk on his lips all but stopped my heart. Fuck, he was so damn gorgeous. The shadows sharpened his proud nose and intensified the heated look in his eyes, and with the way he loomed over me, I was beyond gone for this man.

"Please, fuck me," I said, and Ollie licked his lips. "I just need your cock." My voice cracked, and a flush hit my cheeks as desperation flooded through me. But I didn't care. If I'd only get this one night with Ollie, I needed to come with him buried inside me, like I'd always dreamed of.

"Sinking inside this sexy ass is going to fucking kill me." He pulled his fingers out. I heard the *shlick, shlick* as he lubed up his cock, and a second later, he nudged the thick head against my entrance. As he pushed inside me, sweat prickled across my forehead, and I fought to keep breathing. He was so thick my ass burned as it stretched to accommodate him, and I loved every second of it. The gentle and firm way he gripped my hip grounded me, keeping me from floating away.

Ollie's fingers snuck down and plucked at the elastic of my panties, letting it snap against my hips with a sting that made my cock leak. I was panting as he continued to push in inch by inch, as if he savored the glide.

"These panties are fucking sinful, Liam," Ollie said. "How the hell were you keeping this from me for all these years?" The wonder in his tone broke my damn heart open. I'd been waiting for so long for him to look at me like this, to see the yearning that had been brimming under the surface, and I could barely believe it was happening.

He sank in all the way, and my eyes rolled back. His cock was so thick inside me, filling me to completion, I could die happy. Hell, I'd be willing to stay like this the rest of the night, his body pressed against mine, his cock buried in my hole. However, he began to move his hips, and sparks flew, pleasure sweeping through me.

"Nngh." I moaned, unable to form anything coherent.

"You feel so good, baby," Ollie said, his voice deep and sinful in a way I'd never heard from him before. These aspects of him were ones I'd only ever hoped for but never thought I'd experience. He slid his palms up and down my waist and settled them on my hips as he thrust a little harder.

"So goddamn tight." His nails bit into my skin with how hard he gripped me. "I'm not going to be able to last long with how damn amazing your pretty little hole is."

I let out a whimper, loving how he talked. My balls throbbed with the need to come, and my cock dripped with pre-cum, but part of me didn't want this to end. I wanted him to ride me forever, to take up residence inside my ass so we'd be connected for as long as humanly possible.

My grip on the sheets beneath me tightened, the fabric bunching in my hands as Ollie pumped into me mercilessly. The sting every time we collided, the heady smack of skin to skin, his cock gliding against my prostate in the best damn way—all of it was an intoxicating brew that had me floating higher and higher. Our grunts and moans filled the air, and heat rushed through my body, each breath coming in a little sharper and shorter.

Ollie's big body braced mine, and our sweat-slicked skin rubbed together when he rammed deep inside me with every thrust. My heart squeezed so tight I thought it might fracture, but I rode the bliss coasting over me with Ollie's complete control. He might not seem like the dominant type outside of the bedroom, since he was so damn easygoing, but I'd always suspected he'd take charge.

And fuck, I loved it.

Hell, I'd always loved *him*.

My eyes misted over with the buoyant emotions welling inside me, but I didn't have a chance to dwell on them. Not with the way Ollie had picked up his tempo until those white-hot sparks flared with every pass, and my balls were lifting like I was going to come.

"Fuck, I need to—"

As if Ollie had read my mind, he reached down and wrapped his hand around my cock. "I've got you, baby," he said, the low tone and his callused palm around me all I needed. "Come for me."

It only took two strokes before I obeyed his command.

My balls drew up, and my orgasm barreled through me with the power of a hurricane. I clutched the sheets and weathered the intensity of my release as the pleasure overrode any other senses. My cum splattered on the sheets beneath me, my entire body quaking with the force of my orgasm.

"Oh hell, that feels so damn amazing." Ollie gasped. His thighs tensed behind me, his breath snagged in his throat, and his hot cum flooded the condom. Sweat prickled across my arms, my back, my legs, as we both remained where we were, catching our breaths. My limbs were far too heavy, and I wanted to sink into the mattress, but I couldn't bear the thought of Ollie sliding out of me.

He ran his palm over my hip in a gentle movement, and I swooned. "I know I should be pulling out, but hell, your ass feels so good."

"Don't," I blurted out before I could help myself.

"Pull out?"

"Not yet?" I chewed down on my lip. Should I ask for what I really wanted? I glanced behind me, and my heart thumped a little harder.

Ollie's dark eyes were soft, strands of his chestnut hair pasted to his forehead as he offered me a crooked grin. "Only if I can cuddle you. I came so hard I don't know if I can keep myself upright anymore."

I swallowed hard. This was definitely heaven. "Yeah, I'd love that."

Ollie wrapped his palms around my hips and flopped down onto the bed. When we were on our sides, he swept me into his arms and held me tight like he couldn't get close enough. Even having fallen into the edge of the wet spot I'd left wasn't enough to move me while Ollie's hot breath puffed against the back of my neck and the sweat cooled on my skin.

"I'm just going to park here until you fall asleep, okay? I'll ditch the condom and clean up after," Ollie said.

I snuggled against him, my limbs languid and loose after coming, my mind fuzzy and calm. With Ollie's big frame swallowing me whole and his cock still resting inside me, I felt more at peace than I ever had. My throat tightened with the intense emotions sweeping over me. Of course my best friend would be the one person to understand what I needed.

This sense of completeness was one I'd given up on years ago, one that scared me after how much of myself I'd lost in my last relationship.

And what terrified me more was how this would shatter me once it all ended.

Chapter Ten

Ollie

I was grateful for the cool breeze today.

We were working on a big property, a modern mansion type with asshole clients who liked to nitpick over every last thing, but my mind was a thousand miles away. Every time I thought of what had transpired last night with Liam—the kiss, the blow job, eventually leading to us fucking in his bed—I heated up from head to toe, lust coursing through me. That had been the hottest sex of my life, and after years of barely having any, it was blessed rain on the Sahara.

Since we had a good pre-autumn day rolling through, I worked right outside their garage near the closest electrical hookup. I had the latest section of fencing propped up and was welding new pieces in place of the old, rusted ones. I lit up my torch to work my magic. The beads melted in place as I set the latest bit of steel. The surrounding heat bloomed on my skin, making the work as messy as always, and sweat poured off me. Didn't help that my mind replayed sinking into Liam's tight ass over and over again.

Hell, if I hadn't been wearing a condom, I would've been content to park in his ass the entire night.

Thing was, I was pretty sure he would've let me too.

I fucking adored how much he loved being filled up. It soothed all the neediness inside me for physical touch in a way I'd never anticipated. After years of feeling like I was too much with Josie, who wasn't as into cuddles or PDA, the way Liam and I fit together—fuck, why hadn't I seen our potential earlier?

"You've got a dreamy look in your eyes," Cor said as he approached, like he didn't have a million other projects he could be working on for this house. "Someone got laid last night."

My cheeks flushed something fierce at the comment. Sex was never anything I shied away from talking about, but a few realizations slammed in at once.

He didn't know I'd fucked a guy.

He thought I'd had sex with Josie.

Acid broiled in the pit of my stomach, and I focused hard on firing up the torch again and working on the next piece of the fencing to avoid responding. Everything with Liam had collided together so quickly, like it was some pent-up dam waiting to happen, and we felt so right I hadn't questioned a single thing. But I needed to tell my family Josie and I were getting a divorce, and I dreaded that.

Josie had become such a steadfast part of our family, and she'd gotten close with Aislin and my dad. They would be heartbroken to find out she was moving across the country so they wouldn't see her anymore, and I was scared my family would blame me. I hadn't been as attentive the past few years, since we'd both been focused on our jobs, but part of me started to understand that maybe Josie and I hadn't been right for each other from the beginning.

I finished the piece I was working on and shut the torch off, but to my annoyance, Cor still hung around doing nothing. "Don't you have a job to do?"

"What was it, anniversary sex or something?" Cor asked, clearly not dropping the subject.

"Our anniversary's in February." I said, not knowing how to get around his inquisition. What would my family even think if they knew how fast I'd moved on? They'd be pissed as fuck at me. Worry shot through my veins. What if they were pissed at Liam? I couldn't bear being the one to ruin their relationships with both Josie and Liam, who'd both been integral parts of our family gatherings for years now.

"You know, this whole barely getting laid thing isn't selling married life," Cor said, rummaging through one of our work bags.

"With the right person, it's worth it." All the emotions I'd unlocked last night swelled to the fore again. I'd hammered away at my relationship with Josie for a long time, but the ease in which I'd sank into whatever this was with Liam had unveiled some startling truths. Maybe going through a divorce should've jaded me toward marriage overall, but the intense connection that had sprung to life between Liam and me made me believe in that sort of commitment even more. I'd just been focusing on the wrong person for far too long.

"Sexlessness?" Cor shot back.

"No, married life, you idiot," I responded, setting up the next rail.

"Doesn't sound that great to me." Cor loitered around like we weren't on the job. What my brother wanted was beyond me. We usually did our own thing, tossing the occasional exchange while we worked, but clearly, he was working a problem out.

"Is there something else you needed to talk about?" I placed the shut-off torch down and wiped my sweaty ass forehead.

"I don't know," Cor said, running his fingers through his hair. "There's a guy I met—"

"Wait, you have friends?" I asked, unable to resist.

"Har har. I'm pretty sure he's straight, but he's super touchy-feely. Kind of like you are with Liam. Guess I just needed you to talk some sense into me."

My tongue dried. Yeah, I wasn't the guy to do that—not after boning the fuck out of my best friend. Except Cor thought I was happily married to Josie, and I hadn't even figured out how to open that can of worms with the family. I chewed on my lower lip. Maybe I didn't have to dive into the festering bullshit to still be real with him.

"Honestly?" I said, pausing on the work with the fencing to look at my younger brother. "You'll never know if you don't ask him." If Liam had told me he was interested years ago, would I have taken him up like I had now? Back then, I'd had a set path and trajectory in mind, so I'd leaped into marriage with Josie, but after doing the whole "married with a house and career" thing for years, I couldn't say it had brought me the joy I'd hoped for.

However, this past week with Liam had unleashed a swarm of butterflies I'd missed as well as the passion I'd been searching a long, long while for.

Cor blinked a few times and gave me a scrutinizing stare.

"Maybe he's straight, or maybe he's not, but I'm not going to talk you out of trying if you think there's a chance for something good." I didn't look away, but I sure as hell wouldn't be expanding any further. Coming out to my brother would mean telling him about Liam and backtracking to the fact that Josie and I were no longer together, and that was a whole situation I needed to tackle. And couldn't help but want to put off.

Fuck, everyone would be so goddamn disappointed in me.

"Well, thanks a lot for making me more confused, asshole." Cor shook his head before pushing up from his lean. "Better get back to work."

"It's about time." Thank god he wasn't probing into more. "What are brothers for anyway?"

"Apparently not advice," Cor said, flinging his hand up in salute as he sauntered away.

Before I could get back to work, my phone buzzed in my pocket, and I slipped it out. Josie had messaged.

Can you meet me at the house for your lunch break?

My brows drew together. We'd been pretty chill since our talk, so she wouldn't be dragging me over for no reason. Still, I couldn't help but wonder.

Sure, I'll be there.

When I pulled up to the house at lunchtime, Josie's car sat in the drive, and the familiar sight struck me with sadness. Soon, it wouldn't be in the driveway anymore. Her new job would whisk her across the country in the next few weeks. The timeline was no joke, and I was a little relieved we'd already been drifting for a long while. Otherwise, I would've been shattered by how fast she was moving on.

Turned out I'd moved on just as fast.

I got out of my work truck, my heart thumping a little harder as I thought of Liam. He hadn't been super chatty throughout the day but had sent me our regular messages, which was normal during work hours. I'd been a little worried after everything last night that he'd be freaked out at the big change in our friendship—I might be go with the flow, but Liam was not.

Maybe I should bother him tonight. Take him out? Invite him over?

I walked to the front door and turned the knob. When I stepped inside, all the differences in the house struck me. Josie wouldn't be taking the furniture, but she'd already started moving a lot of her belongings over to her mom's house. Truth be told, I wouldn't miss having Josie's mom around. She'd never liked me much. Still, the empty spaces in the house were a telltale sign of her leaving—most of the paintings on the walls, a lot of the stupid vases and candy trays she would make a big fuss over.

The idea of putting my own mark there made me nervous and excited at the same time. Except I didn't want to be alone in this house.

I wanted a partner here. Hell, I liked being married, having someone to come home to. Maybe that was why Josie and I had stayed together for so long, even though our relationship had lost luster fast.

"Jos," I called out, making my way toward the kitchen. "Jos?" Since I was home for my lunch break, I would need to scrap together a sandwich or something. She wasn't answering, so I shouted out a third time for good measure. "Jooos."

"In here," she called from the kitchen. "For fuck's sake, I'm not Beetlejuice."

Thousands of questions and concerns ping-ponged in my head, revolving around what Josie might want, dealing with my nosy family, and what this new situation between Liam and me meant.

When I stepped into the kitchen, Josie was sitting at the breakfast nook, hunched over the documents she had splayed out on the granite countertop.

I wrinkled my nose. Were we dealing with the house shit already? I thought that was supposed to involve a lawyer. "What's that?"

"The official divorce papers."

I let out a low whistle. "End of an era." I plunked into the seat beside her and began to scan the documents. "Did you think you'd ever be signing these?"

She arched a brow. "Yes. I was the one who asked for a divorce."

I rolled my eyes. "You know what I mean. When we were young and hopeful and shit."

Josie snorted as she continued signing her end of the document. "You're still young and hopeful and shit, and I pray you never lose the attitude, love. We fought a lot because we're different, but that doesn't mean either of our styles was wrong."

I placed a hand over my mouth in a fake gasp. "Are we actually better friends when we're not together?"

"I'd like that," she murmured, pausing mid-signature. "You don't owe me anything, but if you want to keep in contact after I move, I'd always be glad to hear a friendly voice."

"Psh, you better not ask that, or I'll be messaging you as much as I do Liam."

She shook her head, a rueful grin on her lips. "There's no one on this earth you message as much as Liam. I'm glad you'll have him."

I could've sworn she was trying to communicate more, a seriousness in her gaze that felt pointed—or maybe that was my own wish. But she didn't expand upon the line of thought. Instead, she passed the papers my way. "Your turn to sign."

I scrunched my nose and skimmed over the documents before signing by the empty space next to her name.

"What are you going to do with this big open house?" she asked, sitting straighter on the bar stool. "What are your plans?"

I licked my lips as I stared at the document that would officially end my marriage. I liked a lot about my life—my family, my job, my home, my friends. I didn't want all that to start changing in huge ways. Josie was heading off to a brand-new place and a brand-new career, and hopefully, those things would make her happy. It had been clear she hadn't been happy here.

"Guess I'll find out," I said, not knowing what else to say.

Truth was though, I already knew what I wanted.

Liam.

Chapter Eleven

Liam

"We need you to come in this weekend," Maude said, her arms crossed. My shift was almost over, but she'd cornered me in the hall on the way to the breakroom. Bully for me.

I blinked at her, not able to process how she could make these demands. Whenever someone called out or they needed coverage, they didn't ask around and pool resources. No, the director always told me I needed to show up, as if my life outside of work didn't matter. The killer part was that they didn't hold most of the staff to those standards.

Just me.

"I'm not able to," I said, shoving down the flare of my temper.

Maude glanced at me incredulously, all five foot three of grizzled old broad who looked like she chewed on tar for gum and spat tacks at her enemies. "Why? It's not like you've got a partner at home or kids to worry about."

Oh, fuck her.

This wasn't the first time she'd made comments about my lack of the trappings of heteronormative culture, but holy fuck, it made me so angry. I didn't feel the need for a partner. My stint in boyfriends had burned me hard, and kids wouldn't ever be in my equation. But that didn't mean I should get worked to death because they wouldn't hire enough people to cover the shifts. If I ran my own place, I'd make sure we had enough coverage rather than the penny-pinching bullshit I dealt with here.

I heaved out a sigh. Another notch in the "should've opened my own business" category. Maeve would leap on this and build a fucking spreadsheet. I just clung to a scrap of driftwood against the tsunami of changes I'd been facing lately.

"I've got a family thing," I said, even though it was a flat-out lie. I'd been pulling twelve-hour shifts. People didn't last long here, as evidenced by the way Maude blew through PTs, but she refused to hire more, and we'd all felt the burden of her cutbacks.

"Laura's off that day for her kid's recital," Maude said as if that might sway me somehow.

"And I have obligations too." I swallowed the sharpness creeping into my tone. I wouldn't back down on this one. It might be the fact that I wanted to soak in however long I had with Ollie before he snapped out of this fever dream and realized he was straight. Or it could also be because the volume of the little voice—whose name was Maeve—telling me to start my own business had dialed up the volume. Either way, I refused to roll over like I usually did. "So you'll have to find someone else for coverage."

"Careful, Liam," Maude said, her tone so fucking preachy I wanted to knock her over. "We take team player behavior into account when we do evaluations for raises."

Great. Leveraging my pay against me, all because for the first time in years, I didn't want to come in on a day off. I drew a slow, unsteady breath in. "I'm sure my lengthy history with helping out will weigh in my favor."

And hopefully, I'd be done with this fucking place before the next evaluation came up. Maybe I needed to talk to Maeve. The second I mentioned wanting to get the ball rolling, she'd be all over it.

Maude didn't say anything, neither of us budging in this standoff, but I had places to be, and it sure as hell wasn't here. I strode past her and marched to the breakroom, a paste-colored room that reeked of bleach and mildew, just like the rest of the place. We'd been graciously given a shitty microwave that barely worked, a table we'd had to bolster the legs of with duct tape, and a handful of cracked chairs in disrepair. If I owned my own place, I wouldn't treat my employees like garbage. They'd be family.

I grabbed my backpack with my laptop for client notes and slipped the strap over my shoulder. My phone was in the front pocket, and I slid it open, ready to message Ollie. I needed a distraction as soon as fucking possible. And hell, if our hangout turned into anything like the last time, that'd be all the stress relief I needed. The memories of our kiss, sucking him off in the woods, and the way he'd fucked me in bed played on constant repeat in my mind. Never in my life had I had a hotter experience.

The drop would likely wreck me, but I couldn't help checking my texts. He'd already messaged me.

Date tonight?

My heart sped as I stared at two words I'd never expected to see from my best friend. I kept waiting for him to freak out, the shock that not only was he getting divorced but also that he'd started hooking up with me, who was also a guy. Except it hadn't arrived yet. He'd seemed to have already come to terms with what his family and I had realized years ago—that he and Josie were a square peg in a round hole. And he hadn't blinked when it came to kissing or having sex with me. He'd launched into it with a sweet curiosity that had always been pure Ollie.

My heart thudded hard, and I shot a message back.

Sure, whisk me away.

By the time I'd gotten home, showered, and changed into something clean, a knock sounded at my door.

I stumbled as I toed into my shoes, having just thrown on some cologne and buttoned my "fuck me" jeans. I'd tossed on a slutty little blue lace thong in the hopes I'd be getting laid tonight, but even the chance to steal even more time with Ollie had my heart racing faster. Crazy, considering my best friend and I had spent years attached at the hip, especially after I'd moved back to the area postcollege.

The knock made it feel like a date. Normally, he busted into my place like he lived here. I willed my thundering pulse to calm down as I pulled the door open. The sight of Ollie in my doorway lobbed a thunderbolt of lust right through me. He always looked hot as sin with his big, bear frame, the chest hair spilling out of the top of his shirts, and the tattoos and gauges. But after we'd slept together, I found him infinitely sexier. Heat bloomed in his eyes as his gaze raked me over. He'd also put care into his appearance, all scrubbed and clean in a nice form-fitting olive-green tee and khakis that his thick thighs tested the confines of. Combined with his beard nicely oiled and the rich scent of him, metal and whatever woodsy body wash he'd used, and I was in fucking heaven.

"Damn, Liam," he said, breaking the silence first. He stepped in front of me and wrinkled his nose. "Wait, how are we supposed to handle this? I'm used to walking right in for a hug, but I really want to kiss you right now."

"Kiss me."

Ollie closed the space between us, and his lips crashed to mine. He wrapped his hand around my nape with a possessive hold. A silent thrill rushed through me, almost as intense as the butterflies bursting in my stomach. Ollie coaxed my mouth open, sliding his tongue in, hot and desperate as he deepened the kiss, fast turning it filthy. My knees grew weak, and I clutched the fabric of his shirt, sinking into the way he weakened me in moments.

He stole a few more long, languid kisses, then pulled back, and our breaths came out in harsh pants.

"That was a way better greeting," Ollie said, a slow grin curving his lips. Fuck, he was so damn attractive. And having him up in my space like this made it easy to forget all the complications, hell, everything else that mattered.

Made it a little too easy to lose myself.

I swallowed hard as the realization splashed a little ice on my glow, and I stepped back. "So, where are we going?"

"What's the point of a date if you've got all the information? Come on, let's go."

I followed him out the door, locking up behind me, and walked to his Jeep, since he insisted on driving. He kept dropping the word date as we talked, like it wasn't everything I'd been yearning for throughout so many years. We'd only been on the road for a few minutes, right through the thick of town, when he found street parking and pulled into a spot in front of La Taqueria. We'd gotten tacos and burritos here about a million times, and I loved that he'd picked a tried and true for us rather than branching into something fancy that didn't fit.

"Maybe this wasn't the best choice?" Ollie asked, scratching the back of his neck as he cast a nervous glance at me. Holy hell, that was cute as fuck, and my heart twirled in my chest.

"It's perfect. I'm fucking starving."

When we got closer to the tiny Mexican place with its little black awning and bright red door, the scent of cooking meat wafted my way. A handful of picnic tables littered the front, which was where we'd be eating. I pulled the door open, and Ollie slipped his fingers through mine before he led us both inside. My heart marched in double-time. Fucking me behind closed doors was one thing, but this? Claiming me for the world to see? I almost swallowed my tongue as every pent-up, swoony feeling I'd been holding on to since high school surged in like that adrenaline rush of a plane lifting off.

"You want the usual?" Ollie asked all casual, like he wasn't holding my hand in public for the first time.

"Uh, yeah."

As he placed our order, the voices from the other patrons faded into the background. All I could process right now was his palm brushing against mine, our fingers twined perfectly together. In no time, we were already waiting at the counter for our food because Ollie insisted on paying. Sparks lit through me at how he wanted to take care of me. The thought he'd put into this date and the small gestures he showered me with lifted me higher than I'd ever soared.

No wonder no other guy had compared.

"Let's sit outside." I said, casting an eye toward our regular picnic table that was empty. The breeze was a little cooler today, but the waning golden rays of the sun were rich and warm, beckoning me outside. Besides, I wanted our rituals, our familiar. I clutched to them with all my might amid the massive shifts that had occurred in our friendship over the past week. We were changing so fast—ever since Ollie had announced his divorce—yet I didn't want to put on the brakes.

I was strapped into this roller coaster, no matter the outcome.

"Thanks," Ollie said to the guy who delivered over our burritos, covered in foil and guaranteed to be fucking delicious. Ollie passed me mine, unfortunately unlinking our hands. My stomach rumbled at the sight and smell of the savory meat, beans, and cheese. As Ollie walked to the door, I followed him, not skipping the chance to watch Ollie's ass flex in his khakis. After years of furtive glances, it felt so damn good to soak in this man's gorgeous body in action.

I almost tripped from staring too hard, so I clutched my burrito tighter and tore my gaze away as we stepped outside. The early evening sun seeped through my skin, lazy rays compared to the daytime intensity, and we settled into our normal spots at the picnic bench, on opposite sides from each other. Not like I could sit in his lap or mount him in public, but damn, did I want to.

"You have no idea how badly I needed this," I said, tearing open the foil and taking the first bite. As I savored the taste, all salt and grease and goodness, I moaned. When I looked up, Ollie's jaw had dropped, and he just stared at me. I swiped at my mouth. "Is there something on it?"

He shook his head and swallowed, his Adam's apple bobbing. "No, just realizing how hot even watching you eat a burrito is. Like, you've always been hot, but I was with Josie, so it didn't really matter, you know?"

I blinked as my heart stopped and restarted in my chest. "What do you mean I've always been hot?"

"Look, I might have always figured I was straight because I dated women, but I've been aware of your looks for a long time too. I guess that's why none of this is coming as too much of a surprise to me," he said, chewing on his lip. "That's not weird, right? Because of how long we've known each other?"

"Only if having a crush on you for ages is weird." I dropped my gaze.

"Fuck, really?" The sheer excitement in his tone had me looking back up again. Ollie's eyes were bright, and a broad grin stretched across his features. "So, this was inevitable, right?"

My heart thumped hard at his words, ones I could barely process. Sure, I might've sworn off relationships after Hal, but this was Ollie. The fear of losing myself to another guy didn't exist with him because I'd been lost to him years ago.

In truth, it had always been him. I hadn't been waiting around, because he was married, but at the same time, no potential partner could ever measure up to this connection we shared.

Ollie tore into his burrito, and I did the same, enjoying the later afternoon sun, quality food, and the man I adored.

"What were you going to say earlier?" he asked, nudging my foot with his.

"Oh, that." My shoulders slumped. "Just tired of working at Tethered Connections. Maude wanted me to drop everything and cover this weekend with no notice, and she keeps shoving the lack of kids or a partner in my face."

"I've been telling you that's fucked up." Ollie gestured at me with the last quarter of his burrito. A few flakes of rice drifted out. "Do Maeve and I need to strap you down and make you watch inspirational videos about owning your own business for twenty-four hours? Because we'll do it."

I let out a sigh. My folks had said I should too. The only person who wasn't backing me at this point was myself. "How would I even get started, though? When I look at the paperwork, the sheer amount makes me want to toss it all out a window."

Ollie lifted a brow. "You know you're talking to someone who works for a family-owned business, right? Cor and I have already handled most of the paperwork for the business, since Dad's days before retirement are numbered. Say the word, and I'll sit with you, and we can figure it out together."

A lump formed in my throat, and I scarfed more of my burrito to avoid being a total sap. Ollie had always been the best friend I could ever have hoped for, but since he'd started looking at me through a different lens, the potential I saw in him as a partner was so perfect it terrified me.

"Thanks." The first threads of resolve seized inside me. Maybe starting my own business would give me something to hurl myself into when all this fell apart. Ollie and I fit together too seamlessly, and this had progressed so fast I waited for the other shoe to drop.

"Ready for part two of the date?" Ollie said, crumpling his foil into a ball and lobbing it into the closest trash can.

I crammed the last bite of my burrito in and pushed up from the seat. "Lead the way." Ollie could have taken me to a McDonalds, and I'd be thrilled because he'd wanted to go on a date. However, the fact that he showed how well he knew me—the man had completely ruined me for anyone else.

We climbed into Ollie's Jeep, and he blasted his terrible 80s music, and I fucking loved it. We'd only gotten through one of his badly sung renditions of Toto's "Africa" when he pulled to a stop in front of Pets and More. Why were we here? Neither of us owned a pet due to the lack of time to take care of one.

"Did you need to pick up birdseed for your feeders or something?" I asked. The old red-lettered sign had been around forever, as was the big picture of a goldfish they had plastered across the window.

"Come on." Ollie hopped out, being all smirky and mysterious, and strode to the entrance, expecting me to follow. I did.

We walked inside, and he took my hand again as if he couldn't keep from touching me. I swooned at the contact, and my heart accelerated as we headed down the aisle. The scent of wood chips and kibble greeted me, the odd blend that always lingered in pet stores. The place wasn't huge, but it was well known in the area for having a good animal selection, unlike a lot of the stores that just stocked pet supplies.

We'd barely gotten a few steps in when the squawking of birds drew my attention. I always loved looking at the cages, seeing the different types I'd studied over the years. Not like any of the pet birds here were the types I saw while birding out in the wild, but I still appreciated them. "Sadie said they got strawberry finches in," Ollie said.

I perked up at once, moving a little faster down the aisle. "You're kidding me, right? They rarely get more than the normal conures and zebra finches."

"I called just to check, and I figured this would be the perfect stop for us," he said, swinging our clasped hands back and forth.

Goddamn, . I wouldn't ever be able to recover from a single date with Ollie Brannon, because his consideration, the way he knew me better than anyone on the planet, and all of his pure sweetness had claimed my heart years ago.

I squeezed his hand, meeting his gaze. "Thank you," I said softly. "I love everything about our date."

We rounded the corner to the back area where the bird cages were set up, beautiful flashes of yellow and green from the conures, and a few African macaws chattering away in their spot.

Except I zeroed in on the strawberry finches. The tiny little things flitted around, a shocking bright red with black tipped feathers and bright white speckles.

I stole a glance at Ollie and caught the warm glow of his gaze. Hell, the rarest birds in the world couldn't compare.

Chapter Twelve

Ollie

So far, my date with Liam had been the best one I'd ever been on.

It was hanging out with my best friend combined with something more I'd been missing for a long time, and the mix of the two was staggering. I hadn't known a relationship could be like this—effortless and thrilling in the same breath, and while part of me had wanted to keep going somewhere else, I chose to continue our date at my place. Hopefully, he wanted the same thing I did.

A repeat of the other night—any way I could have him.

"Wait, you want to start a playthrough of Final Fantasy X tonight?" Liam asked as we entered my house, which was a lot darker and emptier than I was used to. "I thought you said Tidus was a little bitch."

"He is a little bitch, but it's a fun game—especially if you want to up the stakes," I said, waggling my brows.

Heat bloomed in Liam's pretty blue eyes, and he licked his lips. "This isn't rounds like in Mortal Kombat, so we can't do strip rules.

Although if we took off a piece of clothing for every random encounter, we'd be naked in about five minutes. Or every time Wakka throws a blitzball?"

I snorted, grabbing his hand and dragging him to my living room and the couch, where just last week he'd stripped down for me while playing Mortal Kombat. It felt like ages ago if I were honest—finding out I was getting a divorce and exploring this spark with Liam.

"More of a concentration game," I said, lowering my voice. Hopefully, he caught the drift. Based on how his pupils expanded and he sucked a light breath in, I thought he did.

Sure, we'd only hooked up once, but I'd memorized every single detail about my best friend. And I could already see certain things he liked. He adored having his oral fixation satisfied. The ideas percolated in my brain. Honestly, his fixation meshed with my neediness for contact in the best damn way, and I couldn't believe I'd gone years without this sort of mind-blowing sex.

"Now you've got my attention." Liam closed the space between us in a few quick strides.

I didn't hesitate and tugged at his waistband. "Strip down for me, and you'll find out."

Liam reached down, our fingers brushing as he snapped the button on his jeans and shucked them to the ground. The little blue lace panties stole my attention, and before he could strip farther, I slid a finger along one of the straps, following it around to the swell of his ass, which was mostly bare in his thong. I almost swallowed my tongue, and my cock woke the fuck up. Based on the bulge tucked into the silk pouch in the front, Liam was already turned on too. My mouth watered at the thought of tasting him—I wanted to so badly—but I wanted to fill him up and watch that dreamy expression float to his face even more.

"Fuck, keep them on. You wear these for me?" I asked, my heart thudding harder.

"Yeah, maybe," Liam said, his voice taking on a flirty tone. How had I gone so many years without hearing this aspect of my best friend? This unexplored side of him was one I desperately wanted to learn everything about.

"They're so damn hot." I was unable to help myself from reaching around and squeezing one of his cheeks.

He cocked an eyebrow. "The panties or my ass?"

"Both." Heat pumped through me as I continued to fondle his ass. Liam let out this fluttery little sigh I wanted to devour, so I didn't hold back. I leaned in, my grip firm on his ass, and claimed his mouth. Another whimper escaped him, and this time I swallowed it down as I basked in the taste of his mouth, a lingering hint of the coffee he'd drank on the drive back. He was all heat and passion, melting in my arms as I ground my cock against his thigh while I groped and grabbed at that perfect ass. While I couldn't wait to fuck him again, I hadn't been lying when I said I wanted to explore everything with him—whether it was getting fucked, sucking his dick, sucking each other off, rimming him—whatever.

At those rampant thoughts, my cock grew harder, and I moaned into his mouth as I swept my tongue in to taste him deeper. He began to grind against my thigh, and his stiff length in those panties was turning me on badly. If we kept this up, I wouldn't be surprised if we busted like a couple of teenagers.

I pulled back, my breath coming out heavier. "Okay. Want to suck my cock while I start the game, baby? See how fast you can distract me?"

"Ngh." Liam all but raced over to the couch while I took my time following him. The way his supple ass bounced with his walk had me losing my goddamned mind, and while I might have the game on, I wouldn't be paying close attention to it.

I popped the system on and started Final Fantasy X, a game both of us had played plenty back in the day. The title screen music sounded in the background. I had the controller in hand while I unzipped my khakis and tossed them to the floor. My boxer briefs were next. I sank into the couch and spread my legs, giving my cock a long, leisurely stroke as Liam dropped to his knees before me.

That sight was one I wanted to memorize. The thick strands of blond hair drifting across his forehead, those lush lips slightly open and tantalizing, his slender but solid form, the dusting of blond fuzz on his chest, those darkened nipples, the line of hair leading down toward the waistband of his panties. A little bit of pre-cum dotted the front of them, and I salivated because I wanted to taste him as well. Fuck it. I reached down, slid my hand into the front of his panties, and ran my fingers up his velvet cock, then brushed my thumb across the tip. It felt different from my own but a hell of a lot hotter than I'd anticipated.

Once I captured a bit of the liquid on my thumb, I brought it back up to my lips and sucked. The salty burst on my tongue intrigued me, and I let out a low hum.

"Fuck, that's not fair." Liam panted, the look in his eyes a little desperate, a little crazed.

"You taste delicious. Ready to play?"

"Oh hell yes." Liam's hungry gaze zeroed in on my cock. I gave it another stroke and crooked my finger to beckon him forward. He barely needed the encouragement. Liam leaned in and wrapped his hand around the base of my cock. The moment he licked my tip, a whole-body shiver rocked through me, and I grabbed the controller, trying like hell to get past the title screen. The opening for Final

Fantasy X flashed on the TV, but my focus wasn't on the roar of the blitzball game.

No, my focus was on the gorgeous guy on his knees in front of me, the one with those mesmerizing blue eyes with his lips wrapped around my cock. Liam teased the head of my cock with his tongue, little kitten licks and long, slow circles. The movements zinged through me with force. Going from mostly celibate to hooking up with the hottest person on this earth made it a hell of a lot harder to last. Still, I was a stubborn son of a bitch.

The cutscene with Tidus created a lot of background noise, and the controller might as well have been a prop at this point, as Liam played around, clearly enjoying himself. As he licked over the slit on my tip, I sucked in a harsh breath. He engulfed my length in his mouth, then his throat, and I almost shot up off the couch. My thighs tightened as he began to suck me in earnest, bobbing up and down on my cock. Saliva slid along my cock, pooling on my groin as he swallowed me like this was his final meal. My eyes rolled back in my head, and I summoned every ounce of restraint not to just grip his hair and ride his face until I came.

The plastic controller might crack if I gripped it any harder, and fuck, I'd forgotten how long the cutscenes could be in this game. If I didn't have a distraction soon, I was going to blow my load. The sight of Liam, his mouth stuffed full of my cock, his eyes glassy as he swallowed me down again and again, was apparently my kryptonite. His cheeks were flushed, and his long lashes fluttered as he kept on with his effort. The tight heat drove me insane, pleasure rushed through me, and my balls began to draw up.

The cutscene finally fucking ended, and I fumbled with the controller in a weak attempt to focus on the game. The slight shift reined in my impending orgasm. Barely. Except with the hot suction on my cock, paying attention to the game was nigh impossible, and hell, why would I want to watch that when I had Liam on his knees in front of me? However, the whole arrangement seemed to be working for him as he swallowed me down with a hunger that thrilled me. I loved how he threw his whole self into sex—he wasn't checked out or just ticking a box. No, Liam was so expressive with me, so enthusiastic, and I found myself utterly fucking charmed.

He increased his speed the slightest bit, and that pace would send me soaring within seconds if I didn't stop him. The tension increased a thousandfold, my orgasm barreling toward me at a momentum I wasn't prepared for.

"Okay." I tossed the controller onto the couch and gripped him by the hair. "Okay, baby. Enough."

Liam batted his lashes as he pulled off and wiped his forearm over his spit-slicked mouth, lips slightly puffy. "What? I thought you were paying attention to the game?"

God, I fucking loved this flirty side of him, how it melded with his dry wit perfectly. How had this sexiness been right under my nose all these years?

I leaned forward and ran my thumb across his lower lip, red from sucking on my cock. "Well, it's clear that my concentration's not great, but let's see how you do. Would you rather be sucked or filled up?"

"Filled," he said, his voice a little breathy. We might've only hooked up a couple of times, but I'd noticed how much Liam loved to be filled—his mouth, his hole, whatever. Hot as goddamn sin, and I was happy to indulge.

"Let me grab a condom and lube." He picked up his pants and tugged a few packets out of his pocket. I leaned back against the couch as he pushed to a stand, his knees reddened from kneeling on the carpet. His long, lithe torso, the trail of hair down his chest to the panties he still had on—all those little details cemented in my brain.

"Ditch the panties," I said, my voice a low rumble. "I want to be able to play with your pretty cock while you're sitting on mine."

"Fuck, Ollie." Liam's cheeks flushed as his pupils grew wide with lust. I ran my palm along my length, loving the healthy coating of Liam's spit gliding the way. He handed over the packets, and I ripped open the condom first while he tugged the scrap of fabric he called panties down to pool on the floor. His ass was fucking biteable and right in front of my face, pale, round, and perfect. I didn't bother waiting, just grabbed his hip and sank my teeth into one of the globes.

"Oh god." He moaned, thrusting his ass toward my face.

I bit another spot on his ass, my cock throbbing with the need to drive into him. I fumbled with the packet of lube, spilling a little on my finger, which I then smeared around his hole. Seeing it glistening there, the furled skin darker with some of his light hair around it, I was salivating.

"God, I want to rim you," I said.

"You're going to kill me." Liam glanced back and gave me a flirty wink. "Next time, after I've showered. Right now, I need your cock. Aren't I supposed to be playing a game?"

"Right," I said, spreading his cheek with one hand and then sliding a finger into his hole. The way his hole clutched at my finger reminded me of how goddamn good it had felt around my cock, and lust dizzied my brain. I began to pump my finger in and out of his hole, luxuriating in the silken heat and the squelching sound as I worked the lube into him. Before long, I was adding another finger, and his breaths were coming in a little shallower.

"I'm ready," he said, the neediness in his tone addictive.

"Then come on, baby," I said, pulling my fingers out of his hole. I grabbed his hips, opened my legs, and helped lower him down. "Sit on my cock."

He spread his cheeks wide, positioning himself so his hole brushed against my tip. I sucked a sharp breath in. This was going to be heaven but hell to resist coming my brains out. He sank down, taking his time and moving inch by delicious inch. If I thought he'd felt good before, this position was somehow even better, especially when those lush ass cheeks rested against my groin.

"Mmkay." I reached out to my side for the controller and handed it over to him. "Go make Tidus throw a blitzball or some shit."

"How long has it been since you've played this game?" he asked, glancing back at me, all while my cock nestled snugly inside him. He shifted that sexy little ass the slightest bit. Fuck, this was so goddamn hot.

"Unngh. High school, I think."

"Don't believe you're absorbing much now either," Liam said, amusement in his voice as he picked up the controller and started playing. The character's voices sounded on the screen, and I could hear the click of him hitting the buttons on the controller while I sat here combusting with my cock in his ass. Not moving took every ounce of my willpower. Holy hell, I wanted to just fuck into him until we both were sweaty and sated.

I chewed on my lower lip and spread my legs a little wider to wedge in a bit deeper. Liam's hitched breath was my reward, and while he continued to try and play the video game, I reached around his waist and wrapped my palm around his cock. The velvet length was warm in my hand, and the heft of it felt too damn good. I gave it a lazy stroke.

"Oh god, oh god, oh god," he babbled, the clicking sound of the buttons on the controller ceasing.

I toyed with his cock, bringing my thumb over the tip to the sticky pre-cum pooled there. Damn, that was so fucking hot. I gave the slightest pump of my hips, and Liam let out this strangled noise I adored.

"Come on, don't you want to play the game?" I asked, dragging some of the pre-cum down his length as I continued with a lazy up-and-down slide of my hand around his cock. I hadn't been wrong—it was a pretty cock, all flushed at the tip and with a slight curve to the right. So different from mine, which was thick in comparison with no curve and currently lodged up his backside.

Liam squirmed as I played with him, and the micro-movements commanded my full attention. My cock ached with the need to fuck into him, and I seized on anything at this point. I leaned in and licked a stripe up his neck, then nipped along the cords of his neck.

"Fucking hell. Okay, I give up," he said, dropping the controller to the couch cushion. "Please fuck me."

"Thank god." I kept my firm grip around his cock, but I rocked my hips, driving my length into him over and over. Bliss rocketed through me at a blinding speed at being inside this snug heat again, the smooth glide intoxicating. I was so pent up and not just from being buried in him but also from the sweet suction of his mouth beforehand. And even before, all the time we'd spent together, every brush of our skin, every touch, or every idle kiss got me hotter. Liam burned me up to a supernova, and I was going to explore.

"Oh god, Ollie," Liam sobbed as I began to thrust in harder, moving at an accelerated pace. I couldn't hold back. I let go of his cock and grabbed the opened packet to drag a swipe of lube from it. When I wrapped my palm around his cock again, I tightened my grip and picked up the speed. I hadn't stopped pounding into him from behind, shifting my hips again and again to feel that sweet drag against the tight heat of his ass. The squeeze around my length, the way each thrust sent a fresh burst of pleasure rolling through me, made me want to just fuck him forever.

Except my balls ached, and my cock throbbed, and the need to come turned into a deafening roar. Sweat prickled along my forehead, and I nipped at Liam's neck again, tasting the salt on his skin and inhaling the spicy scent of his cologne. My mind dizzied with lust as I lost myself in my best friend's body, ascending higher and higher than I'd ever thought possible. My nails dug into his hip as I gripped his side with one hand while I fucked up into him, toying with his cock with my other.

His moans grew louder and louder, a melody I wanted to memorize, and the background music of the Final Fantasy game on the TV was sheer perfection. Because this was a collision of everything the two of us had become—casual and fun and comfort, all meshing with the hottest encounters I'd had in my life.

"Fuck, Ollie, I'm going to come." Liam breathed out as I quickened my pace on his cock. I continued to drive into him, the tension inside me coiling tighter and tighter. Except this time I wouldn't hold back. My breaths escaped choppier, my vision fucking shaking with the need that made me tremble. My balls drew up, and the orgasm raced through me before I could stop it a second time.

A roar burst from my chest as I came, the explosion of bliss causing my vision to white out. My cum unloaded inside him, and I tried to keep thrusting, even as my whole body was shaking from the ferocious wave of pleasure slamming into me.

Liam let out a long, loud groan, and his cock throbbed with his release. Cum splashed onto our thighs, dribbling down my fingers. Fuck, that was so hot.

We both sat there for a moment as we came down from the incredible high of our collision, my cock beginning to soften inside him. I leaned in again and brushed a kiss against his nape, and I loved the shiver rolling through him in response. Hell, everything about this date night with him was straight out of a dream. I could never have imagined a relationship like this—full of easy affection and incendiary heat. I'd always only gotten one or the other in the past.

My heart thudded a little harder as immense warmth bloomed inside my chest. I'd always loved Liam. He'd been my best friend from the moment we'd met in high school. However, the way I was feeling now still nestled inside him, my arms wrapped around his torso, his cum cooling on my skin—a depth existed in those emotions I'd never experienced with him before.

The rightness in this moment was staggering.

The rightness I'd spent the entirety of my marriage chasing but never finding.

I pressed a kiss to the side of Liam's neck, three words bubbling inside me that were way too early to unleash.

"Can I just sit here like this a little longer?" he asked, the softness of vulnerability in his tone slaying me.

"However long you want." I settled against the couch. "Grab me a tissue from the coffee table, can you?"

Liam snagged one and made a quick albeit messy cleanup of my hands and our thighs, then deposited the crumpled-up tissues on the coffee table.

I handed him the controller. "Go ahead. Play the game. I want to watch."

He leaned against my chest, my cock still inside him, and I wrapped my arms around his waist, holding him tight. He began to play again, and I rested my chin on his shoulder, alternating between watching the game and him.

Contentment spread through me like a crisp beer on a blue-skies summer day, the sort of perfection you soaked in through brief moments. However, as each moment I collected with Liam stacked, one thing had become very clear.

I was in love with my best friend.

Chapter Thirteen

Liam

I woke up surrounded by muscles and heat, and I didn't want to move an inch.

The memories of last night came rushing back to me—the date with Ollie, returning to his place to fuck on his couch, and spending the rest of the night settled on his lap while he showered me with affection and we played Final Fantasy X together. I'd never had a more perfect night, and it didn't surprise me I'd experienced it with Oliver Brannon. The man was one of the warmest, most considerate people I'd ever met, and having his attention locked and loaded on me was a heady experience.

It made me forget my hesitations, made me throw all my self-preservation out the window.

Ollie's heavy arm draped around me, and he clutched me tight like I somehow might roll away. The heat we were generating was definitely sweat inducing, but I didn't want to budge. The prickles of his beard scraped against my shoulder as he began to move, and the shift of his hips brought his thick morning wood to rub against my ass. Fuuuuck. After the pounding I'd taken last night and how long I'd kept him in me, my ass was feeling it today, but that delicious cock of his was temptation incarnate.

"You awake?" Ollie pressed an idle kiss against the side of my neck. He did that constantly, to the point I was pretty sure I would just float away from how my heart lifted off.

"Yeah," I said, idly grinding my ass back against his cock. Ollie's low moan in my ear was my reward, the hottest sound on earth and one I never thought I'd get to hear. I still waited for the rain to descend, like a shit forecast on a sunny day, but so far, Ollie wasn't freaking out. Instead, he showered me with more affection than I'd received from another guy in years—if ever.

And wasn't that a sad realization? My stomach dropped, and I clutched Ollie's arm wrapped around me a little harder. When this all came crashing down, I knew no one would ever compare to him. I'd sworn off relationships because deep inside, I knew Ollie had always been it for me.

As futile and foolish as it was, my heart had decided a long time ago, and no matter how I'd tried to steer it off course, I'd never been able to convince myself.

"You want breakfast?" he asked, nipping at my ear, then the soft spot between it and my neck. A shiver raced down my spine, and I ground against his length again. "Mmm, or how about I suck your cock? I don't have any plans today, so I'm all yours."

God, if only.

Ollie began to push up on the bed with a creak when a loud bang came from downstairs.

"Olliiiiie," a booming, familiar voice called, and stomping ensued, the racket assuring it wasn't just Cormac who'd arrived.

"Oh, fuck." Ollie vaulted out of bed. He scrambled to find his clothes scattered on the floor. I tumbled from my comfortable spot, my pulse racing as I raced to find my clothes. Shit, I'd left them downstairs last night.

"I don't have clothes," I said, striding toward his dresser.

"Grab something from in there." He yanked on a pair of sweats and a T-shirt. The staircase creaked from the heavy boots of his siblings hitting the treads, and panic rushed through me.

I snagged a shirt of Ollie's from the top drawer and some basketball shorts that would be big as fuck on me, but whatever. I pulled them on and tugged the shirt over my head like I'd started a race. Which, in a way, I had. Ollie's family stomped closer and closer.

"Fuck, fuck, fuck," Ollie said, scrubbing his palms across his face. "I'll go meet them down there."

When he looked up, the apologetic look on his face stopped me cold.

I knew exactly what that meant.

It was every straight guy apology because they sure as fuck weren't going to come out of the closet.

Not for me.

I swallowed hard, bitterness corroding my insides.

"Come down after a minute or two," he said, his brows drawn together in an expression I couldn't decipher. Not while I was falling, falling, falling. Before I could say anything else, he'd slipped out the door and shut it behind him.

Ollie's booming voice clashed with that from the other Brannons. Normally, those noises filled me with warmth and comfort, but not this time. I stood in Ollie's bedroom, the door shut on me like a dirty fucking secret, and my eyes stung from believing for a single minute that this would end up any other way.

What had I expected? Ollie and Josie had just agreed to divorce a few weeks ago. Had I honestly thought he'd shift his whole life around because we had a wild time in the bedroom? Sure, his affection, his sweetness was misleading, but maybe I'd been reading into Ollie being Ollie.

I sucked in sharp breaths, trying to get my head cleared before I had to go out there and pretend I was fine. Like my heart wasn't breaking over this rejection. Ollie wouldn't claim me in front of his family, and hell, I hadn't even given him any indication I wanted more. We'd fallen into this so seamlessly I'd been spellbound.

Except he'd never promised to come out for me or even that this was a real relationship and heading somewhere. I'd latched onto the fact that the boy of my dreams had taken me on a date, and my heart had jumped into the driver's seat and zipped off.

This was why I didn't do relationships—because I lost myself in the process. Hal had been a shithead who hadn't deserved the effort, but even though Ollie was so different, we hadn't had a conversation.

Except my ridiculous, hopeful heart had gone and leaped into the pyre anyway.

I scrubbed my face again, trying to ignore the way my skin crawled and how I needed to escape. There was no reason to stick around. Ollie had his family home, and I would require space for a while after this. Time to introduce some logic into the playing field and forget how this man's kisses consumed me heart and soul.

I drew in a long, slow breath and walked to the door. Their voices traveled from downstairs, making it clear that Cor and Rory had swung over to bug Ollie. I was surprised Rory had gotten up this early, with his usual late-night schedule from tattooing, but I sure as hell wouldn't stick around and find out why. Ollie's house had always been a comfort for me, but after what had just gone down, all I wanted to do was run as far and fast as possible and not look back.

As I descended the steps, I trailed my fingers along the railing, my cheeks burning as a scummy feeling rose in my chest. I hated being a dirty secret in a place I'd always viewed as a sanctuary. I didn't doubt Ollie would want to talk and apologize. And hell, maybe we could resolve this in time, but right now, my gut was telling me to get the fuck out of Dodge and preserve what little pieces of my heart I could cobble together.

As if I hadn't already handed it over to Oliver Brannon years ago.

My skin prickled as I neared the bottom of the steps. The way out the front door was in clear view of the living room, and I'd left my keys and phone in there. Looked like I couldn't just stride out the door and pretend I'd never been here.

I stepped in, and everyone's gazes switched to me. "Hey, guys," I said, not making eye contact, which was sketchy as shit. However, I could barely push through this room with all the memories of last night roaring to the surface, let alone fake a conversation with Ollie and his brothers. "Just gotta grab my keys and wallet."

I snagged them from the coffee table, toed on my sneakers, and hurried to the front door before Ollie or any of his siblings could try and start up a conversation with me. A few comments sounded right as I opened the door, but I'd blurred them out. They could blame my exit on me not hearing what they'd been trying to say.

My throat squeezed tight, and the steep descent from the cozy wake-up this morning rocked me down to my toes. I'd barely made it a few paces before my entire body was quaking from this drop. Those hopes had been ones I'd clutched to my heart for so long that the moment I'd gotten the opportunity, I'd leaped.

Without a discussion, without a question, without a fucking safety net.

But that wasn't fair to either of us. I reached my car, my legs a little shaky as I focused on each breath, each step forward, taking me away from Ollie's.

Ollie was my best friend. He'd always be my best friend. Just because I'd gotten my wires crossed didn't mean we couldn't have the deep friendship we'd always had.

I just needed a little time to clean up the fragments of this broken heart.

Chapter Fourteen

Ollie

Cor and Rory had crashed my perfect morning to settle a debate about fucking hoagies.

Rory insisted the best hoagie was at Elio's Deli, while Cor argued it came from Danny's Pizza. They'd shown up to drag me out and taste-test hoagies and didn't give a damn I had plans that didn't include them. In the past, I probably would've rolled along with whatever. Josie and I hadn't done much together over the last few years of our relationship besides obligatory events.

However, today, I didn't give a flying fuck about their stupid-ass lark. Liam had just raced out my door like I'd hurt his feelings, and I needed to fix it. I wasn't sure where I'd screwed up, but I definitely had. My biggest mistake was not telling my family about Josie yet. Had I even told Liam my parents and siblings didn't know?

Rory blathered on about something, but I'd checked out from the moment Liam hustled into the room and bolted right out. Cor had asked if Liam was okay, but before I could respond, my brothers had started arguing again.

"Okay, but that thick-cut meat is fucking nasty," Cor shot back, gesturing with his hands.

"Whatever, you like thick-cut meat," Rory said, waggling his pierced eyebrows.

My stomach tied in knots. What could be running through Liam's head right now? Fuck—could he have thought I didn't want my family to know about us? They weren't even aware I was getting divorced, and I didn't want them wrongly assuming I was cheating, but hell... My feet itched with the need to chase after my best friend.

Cor rolled his eyes. "Maybe in men but not sandwiches."

"What's the deal with your place?" Rory asked as if he'd just noticed the barren walls and the holes where knickknacks and vases used to be.

"Uh, we're renovating," I lied in a less-than-smooth fashion. My brothers weren't stupid, though. Josie's car wasn't in the driveway, and while she'd been skipping out on family shindigs more often than not over the past few years, she'd made enough appearances people would start noticing. Honestly, I needed to tell Rory and Cor, but not just them. If Mom and Dad found out from my brothers and not me, they'd murder me. Aislin definitely would.

Shame prickled over my skin. I should be confessing about how I'd discovered my best friend was everything I'd ever hoped for in a partner, how I'd wasted years in the wrong relationship to stumble into everything right. Except here I sat hemming and hawing over breaking the news Josie and I were getting a divorce.

At the end of the day, my hesitation wasn't even about my family's sadness at losing her from their lives. I swallowed hard, the guilt flushing through me like I'd mainlined Drano. No, this was all my fucking ego. I'd been the only sibling married, and I'd taken a sense of pride in that, which was one of the many reasons I'd held on for so long, trying to make it work. None of that mattered for shit, though, if I'd hurt Liam.

Because he meant more to me than any bruised ego or pride.

I'd go track him down, and we would talk. Then I would gather my family together and break the news about everything.

I couldn't imagine the alternative.

"Danny's Pizza is known for pizza, not lunchmeat," Rory argued, leaning back in his seat. "It doesn't even hold a candle to Elio's." The sheen of the second skin stuff he put over new tattoos shone on the back of his hand, but I hadn't made out the details of whatever ink he'd just gotten.

Cor shot him daggers. "You just think the guy who runs that place is hot. That's not a good gauge of hoagie quality."

Shit, why was I still here listening to my brothers bicker instead of running after Liam?

"Fine, then let's get our goddamn sandwiches." Rory pushed up from the couch.

My brain still whirled with all the chaos that had descended in such a short timeframe. I'd gone from a cozy morning in bed with the guy I wanted to call my boyfriend and the promise of blow jobs on the table to watch my brothers fight over fucking hoagies while Liam raced out my door like his ass was on fire.

"Sorry, guys, raincheck," I said as I rose to a stand. No way could I stomach anything until I sat down and smoothed out any miscommunications with Liam.

"What, do you have plans with Josie or something?" Cor asked, glancing around the room as if he were putting together pieces of the puzzle all too fast.

"Yeah, got to go meet her for lunch," I muttered, hating the lie on my tongue even as I said it.

Soon.

I'd gather the family soon, and I'd tell them everything. Meanwhile, I had to go find Liam. Rory and Cor were giving me sketchy looks, but I just heaved a sigh.

"Don't you both have a hoagie quest to go on?" I crossed my arms as I waited for Cor to stop lounging around and for the two of them to get the hell out of my house. I loved my family more than anything, but their random bickering could wait.

Liam came first.

While my brothers took their time leaving, I slipped my shoes on and grabbed my necessities, because I'd be following them out. Maybe I wasn't the most aware—especially considering I'd been surprised by Josie asking for a divorce that had been coming a mile away—but I knew Liam. And I knew I'd fucked up.

"See you around," Rory said, clapping a hand on my shoulder before he made his way to the door. Cor tipped a nod in my direction and followed Rory, scrutinizing the empty picture spots on the walls as he went. My stomach might've flipped at the thought of him uncovering my secret, but now I wanted to burst out with the words, if only to get this secret off my chest.

Never in a thousand years would I have expected to get divorced and fall in love again in a month, but then I woke up in bed with my best friend, and yeah. Liam Kelly was it for me.

The door clicked shut, but I was heading out it a moment later. My keys jingled as I locked up, and I hurried to my Jeep. Before I hopped in, I shot off a message to Liam.

Hey, are you home? We need to talk.

Two hours later and all the anxious energy I'd been riding on had deflated.

I'd tried Liam's house to no avail. Neither his nor Maeve's car was in the driveway, and I didn't have a clue what she was up to tonight. I'd also checked the coffee shop they both frequented and struck out there. The coffee I'd drunk sat in my stomach like a brick. After stopping by Anson B. Nixon park and our trail on the off-chance Liam had snuck out there to think, I'd exhausted my list of spots where he could be. My phone remained silent.

Liam was normally fast to answer unless he was at work, so that worsened the queasy feeling in my stomach as I drove around the backroads of Kennett Square, dipping into pockets of Oxford and then over closer to West Chester. I'd been operating on impulse from the moment Liam and I had first hooked up and hadn't even paused to think or talk to him about any of what had been unfolding between us.

My chest tightened as I curved down another winding road featuring golden fields, plenty of oak trees alongside, and the occasional historical markers for different buildings of interest. The sun beamed in through my window, and a sweet breeze rolled through, but it did nothing to cool my anxiety.

I pressed the call button on my phone and tried Liam for the thousandth time, not caring if I came off desperate. I'd always been a needy-as-fuck friend, so if he hadn't been anticipating this response from me, he didn't know me at all.

The phone started ringing, but he didn't answer.

Trouble was, Liam understood me better than anyone. And yes, I wouldn't give up our friendship for anything, but after discovering the dimensions we'd tapped into, the depth of these feelings we could share? I sure as hell refused to backtrack.

Liam's voice came through, but it was only his voicemail, and the beep signaled to record a message.

"Liam, it's me," I said, my heart in my throat. "I'm sorry about this morning. That should've unfolded so damn differently, and if you give me a chance, I hope we can talk. You're the most important person in my life, and I need you in it, always."

I ended the call and tossed the phone onto the passenger's seat. I wouldn't get a call back—not anytime soon. I'd drive around a bit longer to burn off the excess nerves running through me. Pacing around my half-empty house would just depress me. Yesterday, my luck seemed to be changing—the divorce opening the doors to something even greater than I could've imagined.

And Liam was the reason for that.

My best friend might be ducking and running because I'd fucked up with handling my family or because he was afraid or for whatever reason he'd rushed out my door this morning. However, this connection between us was too powerful, too potent, and too damn perfect. I hadn't realized the exact thing I'd been searching for existed under my nose the whole time.

I refused to give up on him—on us.

Chapter Fifteen

Liam

The last place I wanted to be was surrounded by people, but I needed to talk to someone tonight. And Maeve had already gone over to Theo's place, which was why I ended up pulling in front of the big house in Chadds Ford that had been transformed into something infinitely better once Theo started dating Lex, who knew how to handle the heap of repairs needed. The gorgeous Victorian front porch with the picturesque awnings and white railings looked right at home amid the historical spots scattered through the area.

My phone had been blowing up for a while now—all calls from Ollie—and I was so damn tempted to pick up and answer. However, that wouldn't be guarding my heart. The moment he asked me to come over or turned those big, brown puppy dog eyes on me, I'd cave faster than a theater kid trying not to belt out every line of a musical.

My heart ached from this morning, and every time I thought back to the way Ollie had looked at me in the bedroom, the apology in his eyes, the pain slashed deeper. I couldn't fucking handle it. So yeah, I was running and hiding.

I still wore Ollie's clothes, even after I'd stopped at home. Because as much as I wanted to protect myself, the clothes smelled like him—tinges of metal and patchouli—and I couldn't bear to rip my whole heart out quite yet. When I cracked the car door open, I glared on back at the bracing sunshine, which was irritatingly cheery while I was most definitely not.

My mood fit more with bitter rainfall and blasting sad acoustic in the background, but instead, I was making myself talk to other people. Overrated, in my opinion. My heart had hopped in the driver's seat, and I couldn't reason out this situation without an external view. I strode up the walkway to the front door and knocked.

The door swung open, and the scent of cinnamon wafted my way as Theo poked his head through.

"Hey, if you're hungry, I've got some coffee cake left," Theo said, gesturing me to follow him inside. He gave me a quick scan-over, concern flickering in his blue eyes. Clearly, I looked as shitty as I felt.

"I'm not going to turn down your baking." My stomach rumbled, betraying how hungry I was. I should've been at Ollie's house, having orgasms and a late breakfast, but the illusion had gotten shattered when I realized he wasn't telling his family about me. And I'd been through the drill often enough to know what his questioning look meant.

"I might not start the interrogation, but Maeve's going to," Theo said as we entered the kitchen.

"I'm going to what?" Maeve asked. She and Lex were sitting at the breakfast nook in the expansive kitchen, one of the highlights of Theo's house. He should be the one hosting parties more often with how huge his place was, but he'd needed to do so many repairs on the house that his home remained a work in progress.

I swallowed hard as Maeve locked her gaze on me, the scrutinizing "can't escape" one. "Nothing, nothing, tra-la-la," I said, even though my delivery sounded half-assed with how broken up I was. The hollowness in my chest just wouldn't abate.

"Okay, asking to hang out instead of being forced through the door and whatever that"—she gestured at my face—"is means something's going on. Spill."

"Let the man sit down at least," Lex said, dragging a white barstool out for me. Theo had cut a slice of coffee cake and put the plate in front of me. He settled into the one beside his boyfriend, which left me between Maeve and Theo. Great.

I sat, wanting to slump over onto the counter and forget the whole plan of trying to find reason by talking to friends. Reason could suck a ten-inch dildo. Theo's coffee cake taunted me, and my stomach rumbled again. I used the fork to nab a small bite. Cinnamon and sugar exploded on my tongue, along with the rich, buttery flavor of the cake. I savored the brief burst of something good before the weight of this morning descended again.

"You know you're not getting out of here without talking." Maeve leaned against the counter, head propped in her hand, her stare burning like a thousand fiery suns. "You've got breakup written all over your face."

I sucked in a sharp breath and kept my gaze trained on the pretty crumb of Theo's coffee cake. The man knew how to bake. "It's only breakup face if there was a relationship."

"Not like you've ever been forthcoming with the guys you hook up with, but I can make an educated guess that a hookup didn't put that slump in your shoulders," Theo said.

I peeked up at him, then averted my gaze again. The awareness in those hazel eyes pierced right through me.

"Okay, for the dumbass in the room who's not reading all the wink, wink, nudge, nudge, what's going on?" Lex asked, barreling through the way he normally did. I didn't mind. The stark directness reminded me of Ollie, except right now, that made my throat tighten up.

I squeezed my nape. "I can't be blunt about it." Ollie wasn't out, and we hadn't even had the conversation. I wouldn't spill. This was one of the many red flags I should've heeded before I decided to sleep with my best friend, but past me had lost hold of his sanity for a spell.

"Oh, for fuck's sake," Maeve said, her impatience getting the better of her. "So there's a friend you've been crushing on forever, and I presume he finally turned those doe eyes your way?"

I loved and hated my best friend. One of these days, she would be the death of me.

"Fine, yes," I muttered. "We fucked, and he's perfect."

"That was a long time coming," Theo said, his tone soft. My insides squeezed so hard they hurt at Maeve and Theo's expressions, the relief mingled with excitement there. I was about to burst.

"So, what's the problem?" Maeve asked, arching a brow.

"He's straight. It's so new, and he's not out, and I refuse to be in the closet."

Maeve blinked at me and then placed both hands on her thighs. "Liam, Liam, Liam. My sweet, naïve, foolish little munchkin."

I wrinkled my nose. "Please do me a favor and never call me that again."

"If he's fucking you, he's not straight. And besides, he was never straight to begin with. The boy's been giving you heart eyes for as long as I've known him."

I shook my head. "Wrong. He was married—"

Maeve placed a hand up. "And loyal, yes. That doesn't mean attraction just shuts off, and he's always been attracted to you."

"None of this matters anyway," I said, scrubbing my face with my palms. "I don't do relationships."

"What a load of bullshit." Maeve's voice heated in the intense way she got when she was passionate about something. I just wished I wasn't the subject. "You were unavailable because you've been in love with the same man for most of your life."

"She's not wrong there," Theo said, his tone a lot less aggressive, like this was some shit game of good cop, bad cop.

"Man, I should've made popcorn." Lex leaned forward and rested his arms on the counter. "It's always the quiet ones that have the most going on."

I rolled my eyes. "I'm glad my drama amuses you."

Lex flashed me a grin. "Look, I'm not about to step in while Maeve's on a roll. She might murder me."

"*Maeve* isn't done," she said, jabbing a finger at me.

"Ugh, don't speak in third person," I muttered. "It's just douchey."

"You're not derailing this conversation. I've been waiting a long time to see a certain friend of yours get his head out of his ass, and I'm not letting either of you sabotage this. So you're both into each other, but he's not out. Have you asked him what his plans are regarding that?"

My tongue dried, and a wave of embarrassment flushed through me. No, I hadn't. Hell, I hadn't even told him I wanted this to be more. That I'd been in love with him for over a decade. That being together was a long-held dream I never thought would be realized.

I'd jumped to the worst and rushed out the door to protect my heart. And based on the texts, calls, and messages Ollie had left me, he clearly was concerned about what had happened. He'd never been the cruel type, but the moment I saw the apology in his eyes, I started catastrophizing—because I could barely believe any of this had happened in the first place.

"By your lack of response, I'm assuming you two have been fucking like bunnies and not communicating?" Maeve said in her trademarked judgy tone.

"Oh, hey, just like us," Lex said, wrapping an arm around Theo's shoulder and drew him in.

"To be fair, your communication was finding ways to irritate me." Theo cast Lex a knowing look.

"You're the sucker who decided to date me." Lex's grin widened.

Maeve waved her hand. "You guys are passé. We're on Liam pulling his head out of his ass right now."

"Ouch, cruel," Lex said, clapping a hand to his chest.

I shook my head. Thank god for Lex's lightness and how it dragged the attention off me. All the hurt I'd been shouldering today, the steady urge to bolt that had been rising by the second had deflated when Maeve brought up the exact logic I'd been hoping to find in talking to her. After I'd genuinely tried with Hal, I'd been operating in self-preservation mode, and Ollie was the biggest risk to my heart I'd ever encountered.

However, if anyone on the planet was worth the risk, it was him.

I looked up to meet Maeve's eyes, and her lips tilted with a smirk.

"You figured it out, right?" she asked, because my best friend knew me better than I knew myself.

"I might've leaped to assumptions without a conversation," I murmured, taking another stab at the coffee cake. I chewed on a delicious bite, and whether it was having something in my system or the realization that I might've drawn my own conclusions, the ache in my chest began to subside the slightest bit.

Ollie might not feel the same way. He might not want a relationship with me. He might not want to come out.

However, I'd never find out the answer to any of those questions by running away.

"Wait, it's over that quickly?" Lex asked, wrinkling his nose. "Where's the screaming? I thought there'd be at least one plate thrown."

"Okay, but those are one-of-a-kind plates." Theo put his hand on my plate as if I prepared to fling it.

"For fuck's sake, it's a plate," Lex said, and Maeve rolled her eyes. "If it cost more than five dollars, what are you even doing?"

"Where are you getting your plates? Walmart?" Theo shot back.

I met Maeve's eyes and grinned. Those two would be at it for a while. For the first time since I burst out of Ollie's house this morning, the fist in my chest began to unclench.

"Thank you," I mouthed.

She lifted her coffee in Theo's one-of-a-kind blue-and-white mugs in salute.

"What would you do if I jizzed on one of your fancy plates?" Lex asked.

"Probably make you sleep outside," Theo said.

I snorted as I rummaged in my pocket for my phone. The number of missed calls and texts were staggering—all from Ollie.

I opened the first text.

Please, can we talk? I know I messed up, and you're too important to me to let this drop.

I swallowed around the ball that had formed there. Of course he'd be so damn considerate.

Let's talk, I typed back. *Your place in a few hours?*

I didn't put my phone down, and the dots danced almost immediately.

Please. Yes. I'll be here.

My chest tightened, and a sense of the inevitable swept over me, like the feeling of waking up on graduation day.

Maeve stared at me with a reflective expression she only ever wore when she was teaching yoga. "Gonna go get the guy?" she asked as we ignored Lex and Theo who still fought over the plates.

"I'm going to try."

Tonight would determine whether or not I had a future with Ollie, but I wasn't going to run—no matter the outcome.

Chapter Sixteen

Ollie

The moment Liam texted me back, I could breathe again.

Except a couple of hours felt like an eternity while I paced through my house, waiting for the telltale knock on the door that my best friend had arrived.

All I wanted was to curl up with him, to feel his body against mine, because that man was home to me, more than this house, more than my parents' place. Why it had taken me this long to realize mystified me. The signs had been there the entire time.

How I found my gaze straying to him constantly. How I'd taken any excuse to brush up against him or to be near him because I needed his touch. How he was the person I talked to every single day—even more than Josie.

Liam had always been my person, and after wasting so much time not being together like this, I couldn't bear to waste another second.

I scratched my skin, stretched taut and prickly with nerves while I waited. Not like he'd given a specific time, but I wouldn't be able to rest easy until he was in my arms again. All the blank spaces in my house had been taunting me for a bit, but now I saw them for what they were—opportunity. The chance to fill my home with the right relationship, the person who should've been there all along.

As long as Liam was on the same page.

A knock sounded at the door, and I was so keyed up I almost jumped in surprise.

I bolted for the door.

When I ripped the door open, my breath snagged.

Liam's blond hair was swept to the side like he'd put some product in, and whatever body wash he'd showered with smelled so damn good I could catch the spicy scent from here. His blue eyes were guarded and his shoulders braced, but he wore my shirt and the pants he'd borrowed this morning. Hopefully, it was a sign. The slight scruff on his chin, the thick cords of his neck, the way he seemed cool and chill even when he clearly put himself out there—I just soaked up every little thing about him.

"Fuck, I missed you," I said, closing the space between us. I didn't care if I acted needy or threw my heart out on display. I longed to feel his body pressed against mine. My arms were around him a second later, and to my relief, he collapsed against my chest. I squeezed him tight, as if he might disappear, and stood in the doorway, holding the love of my life.

"You know I was just here this morning," Liam murmured against my chest, even as he snaked his arms around my waist and clutched on just as tightly.

"Don't fucking care." I buried my face into his hair and took a long, deep inhale. Maybe I was being a possessive weirdo, but I was so relieved to have him in my arms again. Knowing I'd upset him had gutted me, and I basked in the fact that my best friend was with me now. That I'd have the chance to set things right.

"Can we take this inside?" Liam asked, his voice muffled from the way I squeezed him against my body.

"What, don't want to hang out in my doorway the whole night?" A small smile rose to my lips. The ease with him, how we were able to just sink into our normal rhythm soothed me while also cementing that I would fight for this—for us—with everything in me. Liam was worth the chase, the effort, anything he needed to feel safe and secure. Because if he wanted this with me, I sure as hell wouldn't let him go.

"Okay," I said, pulling away from him only to brush my lips against his forehead. I laced my fingers through his, refusing to drop contact as I knocked the door shut with my heel. "Let's be civilized and sit on my couch."

"Like we've done anything civilized on that couch," Liam said, a lightness in his voice that cast a spell over me.

I snorted. Fuck, last night had been so damn hot. And while I'd been running around all day, I'd gotten the email I'd been waiting on, one that made me even hotter with the possibilities.

However, now wasn't the time to bend Liam over the couch and fuck him until we both came. Now was the time to have a real talk about everything that had unfolded between us—whether my best friend liked it or not.

"Okay, so I have to tell you something," I said, leading him over to the couch and all but dragging him onto my lap. He sat next to me instead, our legs touching and our fingers still threaded together. Liam's Adam's apple bobbed. No matter how chill he acted, he was nervous too. I held his hand tight. "I haven't told my family about Josie yet. And no, not because I'm holding on to anything, but part of me didn't want to rock the family by telling them she'd no longer be a part of it. And the other part was just me being afraid of disappointing them. Because I'd failed to make my marriage work."

Liam opened his mouth as if he were about to jump in, but I squeezed his hand and kept on my roll before I lost my nerve.

"So that's why I was a shit this morning about going downstairs with my brothers. I don't want you to think I'm keeping you hidden or anything or that I'm not serious or whatever caused you to run out my door." I swallowed, my chest tight at the intense feelings I tried to hold back from exploding out of me. Liam might go running for the hills after all this word-vomiting, but I couldn't stop myself. "Yes, this is super early and right after a divorce, and we just started doing, whatever this is, but I already know you're it for me."

Liam blinked, opened his mouth again, then shut it. I was buzzing while I waited for his reaction. Would he bolt out on me, blanch in disgust, or tell me I'd gotten everything wrong?

"What...do you mean by that?" he forced out.

I frowned. "By what? I know it's stupid I haven't told my family about Josie yet—"

"No, about us, you dipshit," he said, the slightest hint of a grin tugging at his lips. When he looked up at me and our eyes met, the blaze of hope that emanated from his was so spellbinding I could barely process what he'd asked. He bared his entire soul to me, all his vulnerability on display, and fuck, I'd never loved him more.

With Josie, I'd spent thirteen years trying to make us work.

With Liam, it had always been effortless.

"I love you," I blurted out, not holding anything back. Not with him. "And I don't know what you want out of this thing between us, but I just want you, in whatever way I can have you."

Liam swallowed hard, and his eyes began to gloss. "Oh fuck," he said, his voice coming out shaky.

My eyes widened, and I brought my free hand up to his cheek. "Are you okay? Did I say something wrong?"

"I've loved you since I was fourteen years old, Oliver Brannon," Liam whispered, the intensity of his words settling in my limbs. "You have no idea how long I've been dreaming you'd tell me that."

"Well, about fifteen years, if I'm doing the math right." Giddiness bubbled up inside me.

Lips twitching, he lobbed a light punch to my shoulder.

That emotion blooming in his eyes was rarer than spotting a white wing tern, and I'd treasure that look for the rest of my life. Liam had always shielded his emotions, trying to squirrel them under a protective shell, but now, he blazed with everything he'd been holding back all this time. My heart lurched like it no longer belonged in my chest. It clearly didn't.

Liam had always owned it.

Our lips found each other's, and I wrapped my hand around the back of his head, my fingers tangling in the short strands. This kiss was everything I'd been craving—the sort of passion I'd dreamed of, the thrill of an adventure, and the safety and warmth of home. Liam's lips met mine again and again as if he, too, couldn't get enough, and I pulled him closer, tugging him onto my lap. We barely broke for breath as we maneuvered, but he straddled my lap, and the weight of him made me complete.

For minutes, hours, who knew how long had passed, I just kissed the hell out of the man I loved. His mouth was addictive, and the coy way he'd nip at my lower lip when he wanted me to get more aggressive set me on fire. I gripped his ass, needing to feel him pressed against me completely. The sheer, sunlit joy bursting inside me was the opposite of every ounce of fear I'd experienced this morning, and I unleashed all of that as I swept my tongue into Liam's mouth, swallowing his moans.

When I finally pulled away from him, we were both gasping for breath. His lips were puffy, red, and spit-slicked, my fucking favorite, and I reached up and traced the lower one with my thumb.

"Together?" Liam asked

"Huh?"

"To answer your question, I want to be with you too. Dating, boyfriends, whatever label you want to put on it," he said, those long lashes fluttering as he glanced to the side.

Giddiness returned full force, and I couldn't help the broad smile that broke out over my face. "Boyfriends, definitely. The next time I'm with the family, I'm breaking the news about Josie, and then we'll tell them about us. No more sneaking around, okay?"

Liam swallowed hard, those blue eyes going a little glassy. "Yeah, I want that."

Truth be told, boyfriend was a little flimsy compared to the intense way I felt, but he'd tell me to calm down if I confessed I wanted him to be my husband. Yes, my divorce hadn't been on my horizon a month ago, so it was insane to be even considering that. However, we'd wasted so much time getting to here that I wanted to race ahead and enjoy everything.

At least we could start with one thing specifically.

I fished my phone out of my pocket, swiped it open, flipped to the results I'd been waiting for, and flashed them to Liam.

"I got tested a few days ago. Negative."

Liam chewed on his lower lip, heat flooding his gaze. "So, what you're saying..."

"If you want to go bare?" I asked, my pulse speeding up.

"Oh hell yes."

Chapter Seventeen

Liam

The day had completely flipped over from this morning.

Ollie grabbed my hand and led me to his bedroom. Going bare wasn't something I did with anyone. The guys I slept with were one-night stands, but I'd definitely had a lot of filthy fantasies revolving around it. Of being fucked and filled and staying that way for as long as possible.

And it was fitting that the only person I'd be doing that with was the guy I'd gotten boners over for years when we crashed at each other's houses in high school. The one who'd brought a six-pack of Victory beer when I had a rough patch, and we'd game for hours until the issues drifted away. The guy who'd sent me pictures of the birds he spotted every single day, just because.

Ollie had always been the closest person in my life, but the moment we'd unlocked the door on more...goddamn, this was better than any fantasy I'd ever entertained.

When he nudged open the door the rest of the way and whisked me into his room, I was transported back to the ease and comfort of this morning. Ollie was always a source of warmth and happiness, so open and earnest compared to my closed-off, curmudgeonly self.

"Holy hell, I need to be inside you." He stepped toward the bed. "Though I wouldn't mind the reverse in the future. If you're open to it."

I licked my lips. While I had my preferences, I'd be happy to give him the experience. "As long as you're aware I'm the slutty bottom in this relationship."

"Oh, trust me, there's no way you could stop me from fucking that sweet ass of yours."

"The romantic things you say."

"You want romance?" Ollie said, grabbing me by the hips so we were standing flush against each other. "Loving you is as easy as breathing, Liam Kelly, and I don't know how I missed this connection for all these years."

I placed a palm over his heart, the steady *thump, thump, thump* soothing. "I think a part of me was always waiting, even if I didn't want to acknowledge it."

"Well, now that the wait's over, you've got me for as long as you'll keep me," he said, those soft brown eyes fixed on me.

Forever was on my tongue, but it felt too immense to say it. His lips quirked with his grin, his gaze knowing, and I could tell he understood regardless.

"But right now, I'd love to suck your cock." I licked my lips.

"Only if I get to sink inside you after." He arched his brows with the sinful wickedness he displayed in the bedroom. Outside of it, the man was bright and captivating, but in private? Goddamn, all the heat and energy concentrated on said target—me.

"I'd be disappointed if you didn't," I said, dropping to my knees beside his bed.

The jangle of Ollie's belt traveled to my cock, a zing I couldn't deny. I opened my mouth, sticking my tongue out and looked up. God, I loved the view. Ollie's T-shirt stretched tight over his shoulders and barrel chest, and I wanted to bury my face in his neatly trimmed beard. He stared at me with the sort of heat that rushed through my whole body, which vibrated with need.

He pushed his boxer briefs to his thighs and ran a hand along his prominent erection. I'd already memorized the heft of it, the feel, the taste in our first encounter, and saliva pooled in my mouth at the thought of blowing him.

"God, you look so fucking hot on your knees," Ollie said. "Come on, baby, suck me down."

I all but lunged for his cock.

I wrapped my hand around the base and guided the tip into my mouth, the salty burst of his pre-cum on my tongue. His cock felt like velvet and filled me in the best damn way as I closed my lips around his length. Once I'd gotten a few inches in, I began to suck, getting it nice and wet. The saliva eased the glide as I took more and more of him until he was halfway down my throat. Ollie gave slight thrusts of his hips, and I relaxed my throat to let him use me.

A loud moan ripped through the air, and Ollie's fingers threaded through my hair, finding a tight grip I loved. I bobbed up and down on his cock, saliva pooling around my mouth, dripping to the floor. I could suck on him forever and never get tired. The weight, the thickness, how it made me feel possessed, claimed—hell, I could fall asleep with his cock in my mouth and be blissfully happy.

I continued to suck on his cock, loving the sting as he tugged my hair a little tighter, as he fucked into my mouth a little harder. My eyes fluttered shut, and I floated along the blissful sensations.

"Your mouth is too fucking good, baby," Ollie said, his voice ragged. "I'm going to come if we keep this up."

He yanked me back by the hair, and a sound of protest escaped me as he pulled his cock out of my mouth.

"Strip for me," he said, delivering the order like he was born for it. For such an easygoing guy outside the bedroom, he was so fucking commanding here. Better than my wildest daydreams.

I wiped at the spit around my mouth and dragged the shirt of his I still wore over my head, followed by dropping the pants. I hadn't bothered with underwear, which served me perfectly now.

"On the bed, baby," Ollie said, giving me a long, lascivious once-over while he shucked his pants and boxer briefs to the floor. "Grab the lube and work yourself open for me."

I sucked in a sharp breath. God, bossy Ollie was so damn hot. My cock throbbed with neediness after having his length in my mouth, and I absently palmed it.

I snagged the bottle of lube from the nightstand and spread myself out on his bed, the rumpled sheets beneath me still smelling like us. I widened my legs and clicked the bottle of lube open, then squirted some onto my fingers. Ollie ripped his shirt off, and the furious blaze of lust in his gaze made me hot all over. I smeared lube around my hole, getting my fingers nice and slick before slowly plunging two inside.

"Nngh," I moaned as I began to pump my fingers.

"Fuck, you have no idea what you do to me," Ollie said, his voice wrecked and hoarse. "You're the hottest thing I've seen in my life, Liam." He approached the bed, each step deliberate, and when he climbed on top of the mattress, the creak and movement sent a jolt of anticipation through me. He was going to be inside me—no barriers between us.

As I fucked my fingers inside me, the wet *schlick* echoed through the room.

Ollie situated himself between my legs and skated his big palms along my hairy thighs. He dragged his thumb down the hollow of my hipbone, eliciting a shudder from me. My cock was hard and leaking, but he wasn't paying it any mind as he brushed those callused fingers across my hips, my legs. His gaze focused solely on my fingers tunneling in and out of my hole, the lewd noises making his nostrils flare.

"You're going to feel so good I'm never going to want to leave," he said, grabbing the bottle of lube. He opened it with a click, and a second later, he was slicking up his cock with it. My breaths grew a little faster as I quickened the pace of fingering myself open. I needed his thick length inside me with a desperation that coasted across my skin, making it feel too tight, like I might leap out of it.

"Please," I begged, and he nodded, dragging my hand back.

With Ollie settled between my legs, his cock inches away from my hole, a sense of the inevitable settled over me.

I was meant to be his, and he was meant to be mine.

Some part of me had always known it. Connections like this were rare and precious, and I'd hold on to ours with all my might.

Ollie brought the head of his cock to my hole, and as he entered me, the burst of feeling from skin to skin was pure electricity. I was nice and open for him, so he slid in with ease. Fuck, this was everything I'd hoped for. The slick glide of him, the velvet heat of his cock as he stretched me even farther. My eyes rolled back in my head as he bottomed out inside me, and for a moment, neither of us moved, basking in the intensity of being joined like this.

"Motherfucking hell, baby," Ollie said as he wrapped his hands around my thighs. "You feel like sin."

And then he began to move.

The thin layer of the condom had never seemed like a lot before, but oh god, the sensations were so much stronger without it. A loud moan ripped from me as he dragged his cock back and shoved it forward again, building up steam with the rocking of his hips. He had a tight grip on my thighs, his nails imprinting on them. Each time he snapped his hips forward, driving his cock deep inside me, he grazed across my prostate. The flare of lust over and over and over was driving me out of my mind.

I drank in his scent, metal and patchouli, and sweat beaded on my forehead and chest as he fucked me harder. My hands were splayed above me as I surrendered to the way he worked me over, rocking up to meet him with every thrust. The feel of Ollie deep inside me tugged at the connection again, the one that had snapped into place so many years ago.

This man was so much of my past, and now, he was my future.

Ollie's breaths came out harder, a slight sheen covered his skin, and his chest hair was damp. He moved at a quicker pace, hitting my prostate more and more frequently. The pressure had started building with each stroke, and bare like we were, I felt all of him. I fucking adored it.

"You're so damn tight, baby," he said, his voice ragged. "You feel so damn good."

"I want you to come inside me." I needed it so desperately. The throb of his cock, the salt of sweat and the tang of blood from my swollen lips, the steady slap of our skin as we collided pushed me closer to the brink. This experience was raw and heady, making my mind swirl, making my whole being vibrate with the need for release, to feel his cum gush inside me.

His grip on my thighs kept me pinned in place as he drove harder inside me, each thrust vaulting me higher and higher. My moans exploded out of me, wanton and loud, mingling with his as we raced toward a finish line I never wanted to reach.

I just wanted to live in this space right now, our bodies joined, moving in unison as pleasure flooded through me with every stroke of his cock.

"Fuck, you feel too amazing." The cords of his neck strained, and he clenched his jaw. "I've got to come."

I grabbed my cock and started pumping my fist up and down it. I was so keyed up all it took was three strokes. The tension that had been coiling tighter and tighter exploded.

My balls drew up, and I came so hard I blacked out.

Hot cum splattered across my chest as pleasure flushed through me in a fierce sweep, stealing my senses. Ollie never stopped fucking me, my body rocking with his desperate thrusts. Based on the groan escaping his lips and the way his nails were biting into my thighs, he was close.

Ollie let out a deep, low sound that rumbled through me, and his cock pulsed as he came. The cum flooded inside me with a surprising heat, and my eyes rolled back in my head at how much that turned me on. I was spent as fuck, so my cock wouldn't be rising anytime soon, but I bit my lip. Nngh. God. If he wanted to come in me every day, I'd fucking let him. Hell, I'd roll out the welcome mat and invite him in.

Ollie collapsed on top of me with a grunt, smearing my cum between our chests. His weight was heavy, and I lazily flicked him in the side.

"I'm not moving." He leaned down and nipped at my ear.

"I do need to breathe," I said, flicking him again. My limbs were loose and heavy after coming so hard, and I wanted to lie here in bed with him for the rest of the evening. Hell, into the night.

"Fine, I'll move," he said, maneuvering us onto our sides. A little thrill rose in me that he was still buried inside me, and I hoped he didn't have any plans of pulling out anytime soon.

"You know the cum is going to crust." I glanced at the small space between us. He drew me in closer and buried his face in my neck, something he seemed to do frequently. I loved the gesture, the closeness, and the intimacy of it every time.

"I don't care. You walked out the door earlier, and we hadn't discussed any of this, and I was terrified I'd screwed everything up. I can't lose you, Liam."

His arms were wrapped tight around me, and as much as I'd been afraid of losing myself in someone else for years, those fears didn't even manifest around Ollie. We were so intertwined, our histories richer together, that it never mattered.

"You won't," I said, my voice trembling a little. "I'm not going anywhere."

"Good," he said, the word a bit muffled as he spoke into my neck. "Because you're all mine now. And I'm going to spend as long as possible buried in you tonight—not only because I think you want that more than you're going to admit, but hell, I just need to be connected like this for a while more."

Our limbs tangled together, the room quiet apart from the steady sound of our breaths, and we were burrowed so close I felt the *thump, thump, thump* of his heart against mine. The truth surged within me, and unlike so many years when I'd had to keep those feelings tamped down and buried, I let it rise to my lips.

"All I've ever wanted was to be yours." I closed my eyes, basking in the perfection of this moment.

Chapter Eighteen

Ollie

"**W**hy's your family doing brunch?" Liam asked as he pulled on his sneakers.

We'd stayed in bed last night, cuddling and watching old Star Trek episodes until we passed out. Even as my cock had deflated, I'd stayed inside Liam for as long as possible, and being together with him like that, having him wrapped in my arms—fuck, I was the happiest I'd ever been.

"Who knows the ways of the Brannons," I said with a shrug, waiting by the door. Nervous energy buzzed through me at the thought of telling my family everything, but I wouldn't get a better opportunity than this. I'd have to volley a lot of information at them at once, and chances were I'd blunder through it. However, Liam was the most important thing to me, and I didn't want to spend another day without everyone knowing the joy I'd found.

Even if they all thought I was insane for leaping out of a marriage and into a new relationship.

Which would probably be the case.

"Hey, what's going on?" Liam asked, smoothing his fingers over my brow. "You look like you're thinking, and that's never a good sign."

I rolled my eyes. "Thanks, asshole."

"You don't have to rush to say anything—" Liam said, his blue eyes clouding over. I hated that expression, like he believed I might want to hide him away.

I shook my head. "There's no reason to keep us quiet. I was just protecting my stupid ego with not telling them about the divorce."

"I meant about coming out." Liam gave me a pointed stare. "You've got to be the most chill person on the planet to go from straight to bi."

"You've always been hot, though. And it's not like I got the chance to explore my sexuality in high school or college, since Josie and I were together so early."

Liam snorted, but the affectionate gleam in his light eyes burrowed into my heart. "Never change, Ollie."

"Not planning on it," I said, reaching down for his hand. He gave me his palm automatically, and our fingers entwined. A happy little shiver traveled through me as we walked out the door. I didn't even pull my hand away to lock up, managing it all with the other while Liam watched on, amused. We made it to my car, where I reluctantly gave up his hand, but when we both settled into our seats, and I started the ignition, his palm rested on my thigh as if he knew how much I needed the touch.

The hum of the engine mirrored the rumbling inside me, the pent-up energy converting to action. I pushed the gas pedal, and off we went, only a few minutes away from my parents' house. Some days I even walked over, but today I needed the security of a getaway vehicle, just in case.

When we pulled to a stop in front of my folks' place, I was surprised everyone's cars were already there. I'd thought it might just be my parents and a sibling or two, but Aislin, Cor, Declan, and Rory had all arrived.

Which meant the spotlight would be on me and Liam. My throat went dry.

"You've got this," Liam said, squeezing my thigh. "And if you don't, that's okay too. I'll do whatever you need me to right now."

That, if anything, bolstered me. The fact that Liam was willing to put his heart and hurt on the line confirmed I'd be telling my family today. Not only that I was getting a divorce, but also that I was bi and dating my best friend.

Either they'd rejoice or...well, I couldn't think of the alternative, or I'd freeze.

"Let's go," I said, tugging the keys from the ignition and setting off down the walkway. My palms were sweating, and nerves prickled through me. My folks had two bi kids and a gay son already, so it wasn't like they'd hate me for that. Still, revealing something so personal peeled away any armor. Declan would be the last straight kid left in the family.

A hysterical laugh bubbled inside my chest, and I wasn't able to catch it before it escaped.

"You okay there?" Liam placed a hand on my shoulder.

"Yeah, dumb thought," I said, biting back another cackle as if that might eradicate my nerves. "I'll tell you about it later."

We reached the front door, which stared down at me menacingly. Showtime.

When I pulled it open and stepped inside, the whole family was waiting for me. While I knew they were all here, what I hadn't expected was for them to be crowded in the living room and fixating on me as soon as we entered.

The hushed quiet was even weirder.

Normally, stepping into the Brannon household was a recipe for chaos—loud voices, people walking around, sometimes impromptu house projects. However, my family all in the same space, not moving and being quiet for once? Yeah, alarms were going off big-time. Liam bumped into my back. I'd stopped midstride upon heading into this Invasion of the Bodysnatchers version of my family.

"Okay, what's going on?" I asked.

Cor and Declan whisper-hissed, both trying and failing to argue about something under their breath, and Mom and Dad glanced between each other with worried looks. Before either of them could say anything, Aislin pushed up from the couch and marched toward us.

"Sorry you're here for this, Liam. Chances are you already knew anyway."

I wrinkled my nose and braced myself, not moving any closer because guaranteed they'd figured out one of the myriad secrets I kept from them at this point.

"I ran into Josie at the grocery store the other day," Aislin said, arching a well-defined brow.

Ah, that.

"When were you going to tell us you were getting divorced, Ollie?" Mom asked, a hint of hurt in her voice that burrowed right into my chest. The concern that tilted her brows and the sadness in her and my dad's eyes got to me, and the words spilled out.

"I meant to when it happened," I said. "But that was only a few weeks ago, and a lot has changed since then."

Like realizing I was bi and dating my best friend.

"So the reason your house looks like it got tossed over..." Cor crossed his arms in an attempt to look intimidating, but he was my little brother and would always fail in that regard.

"Is because Josie's at her mom's. She's getting ready to move across the country for a new job, so we've already started splitting everything up." I walked farther in and glanced back to make sure Liam was following and hadn't bolted out the door to safety. He stood behind me, his blue eyes serious and his whole being buzzing with nervous energy. Chances were he was thinking of a million ways this could end in disaster and how I would chicken out of telling the family about us.

He was wrong.

"Okay, how did this all even come about, though?" Declan asked. "You guys were fine."

"I mean..." Aislin passed a glance to Mom.

"What was that?" I said, pointing between the two of them.

"Look, we're not blind, son," Dad said.

"I mean, Declan wasn't aware, but he's the only one," Rory drawled, leaning back in the recliner.

"What the fuck are you on about?" Declan shot him a glare, but I was already well into the room and doing the same to my family. Apparently, the lot of them had plenty to say about my marriage.

"Going to fill me in?" I asked Cor. He was the softie who'd cave first.

"You guys have seemed distant for the last few years," he said, scratching the back of his neck. "Most of us were wondering if this was coming, that's all. Before, you used to argue a lot, and I dunno if that was your thing or whatever, but it changed."

"I'm glad everyone felt the need to fill me in." I crossed my arms. Irritation prickled through me that they'd all seen something that had taken Josie asking for a divorce for me to understand.

"Hey," Aislin said, placing a hand on my forearm. "We just didn't want to upset you. But we wanted to know why you hadn't told us and if you're even okay after she dropped all that on you."

The annoyance melted from me at those eager expressions of concern, apart from Declan, who looked disgruntled that no one else was surprised about the divorce. Instead, amusement welled in my chest to replace those feelings. They might've seen the divorce coming, but they wouldn't have guessed the other part.

"I'm better than okay," I said, a giddy smile rising to my lips. The secret about my divorce was out, and it felt ridiculous I'd even hid the news that long. Riding on that adrenaline, my nerves completely disappeared, and I grabbed Liam's hand, interlacing our fingers together. "In fact, I'd like to introduce you to my new boyfriend."

Mom and Dad blinked at me as if they were trying to process the news. Aislin cocked her head to the side while Cor and Rory glanced to each other like they attempted to confer through telepathy. Declan shrugged.

"This is how you're telling them?" Liam hissed by my side, shooting me a panicked look.

Sunlight filtered through my insides, and I let out a bark of a laugh at not only my family's shocked expressions but the sheer relief of having all the weight off my shoulders. I'd never been good at keeping secrets anyway.

"It's new, obviously," I continued, squeezing Liam's hand. "But he's the one for me. Josie did me a favor, because I never would've realized what I already had here if she hadn't asked for a divorce."

Declan's brows drew together. "This is what everyone's shocked over? I thought you guys had something going on for years, an agreement with Josie or whatnot."

"No, this is new."

"I mean, not on my end," Liam said.

"Well, that's always been obvious," Rory said. "Though Ollie being a part of the Q Crew is a twist I hadn't anticipated."

"Don't call it the Q Crew. That's the worst fucking callback," Cor shot back.

"Wasn't that some old radio station thing?" Aislin asked.

"Thanks, children," Mom said. "You make me feel like a dinosaur."

"Our sweet, loving brontosaurus," Rory said, earning himself a glare from Mom.

"So you're with Liam now?" Dad said, thankfully drawing us back to the point I'd been trying to make. His expression wasn't clear, but I'd already bared everything, so I bulldozed through.

"I am, and I hope you all will welcome him into the family," I said, letting go of Liam's hand to wrap my arm around his shoulder and pull him against me. It hadn't been enough contact, and I was needy, so sue me.

"Ollie," Dad said, his eyes crinkling at the edges as a slow grin rolled to his face. "Liam's been part of the family for a long time. I'm glad he's not going anywhere."

Relief crashed in at those words.

"Thanks, Craig," Liam said, his voice thick.

"Fuck, this makes so much sense." Aislin bounced on her heels. "You guys have been attached at the hip forever, so it's not like you can get even closer."

"Oh, we definitely can," I said, waggling my brows.

"Knock it off," Liam muttered, elbowing me in the side.

"Yeah, if I can't talk about my one-night stands at the breakfast table, you don't get to talk about your gross committed relationship sex," Rory shot back.

"You kids keep this up, and I'm going to chime in with my sexcapades," Mom said.

"Oh god," Declan said, rising from the seat and heading toward the kitchen. "Never say sexcapades again."

"La, la, la." Aislin plugged her fingers in her ears as she followed Declan. "I'm going to grab some coffee. We might as well dig into brunch now that the interrogation's over."

"Intervention," Cor said. "It was supposed to be an intervention, but no one would let me put up a banner."

"Interrogation seems more accurate with you lot," Liam said, still curled against my side because he fucking belonged there. I squeezed him a little tighter, my heart expanding so big I thought it'd explode in my chest.

Mom caught my gaze and winked. "I'm happy for you."

I beamed back, so damn overjoyed at what I'd found. After years of trying to make my marriage work when it had always been not quite right, this was breathlessly easy in comparison. Not like we wouldn't have our hurdles down the line, but Liam and I clicked, the way Mom and Dad did—the way I'd always hoped for in a partner.

"Wait, if Declan's in the kitchen, there's not going to be any bacon left for the rest of us," Rory said, shooting from his seat like his ass had caught flame.

"Man likes his meat," Cor said with a smirk. "Are we sure he's not bi too?"

"Might as well collect a full set at this point." Dad glanced at Mom. "Do we have an ability to just produce queer kids?"

"Or your sperm's really gay," Mom said with her normal quick wit.

I snorted. "Okay, let's get food before everyone else devours it. All this interrogation is making me hungry."

"Everything makes you hungry," Liam said.

I leaned in close as we walked toward the kitchen. "You always make me hungry."

The shiver rolling through Liam was the only reward I needed, but the way he bit his lower lip was a bonus. This man was so damn hot, and he was all mine. Before we stepped into the kitchen, I placed a kiss on the top of his head.

"How are you feeling?" I asked. "With everything out in the open?"

He looked up at me, those blue eyes glossy. "I'd dreamed about it for so long I never thought this would happen in real life. Thank you."

"For what?"

"For being worth waiting for." Liam pressed a kiss against my cheek. The tenderness of the motion sent a thrill through my heart, and I clutched him even tighter, wanting to drag his body against mine any chance possible.

"No one asked for this gushy display of affection," Rory called out. "Either get your asses in here or find somewhere private."

"Maybe we should've kept our relationship quiet longer," Liam muttered, and I snorted out another laugh.

"Yeah, like that would work with this nosy bunch. Just wait until we tell your friends," I said, elbowing him in the side.

"They're aware," he said as we walked into the kitchen. "I never named names, but Maeve's had your number for years."

"Oh good. That'll make next game night a lot easier."

Liam shook his head, trying to play it cool, but his dopey grin was one I wanted to memorize. The way his pretty blue eyes gleamed, how his normally guarded expression lit up. My heart responded in kind as if some instinctive part of me had always known he was mine.

"Were there cinnamon rolls?" Rory asked Aislin, who nibbled on one. "Because I'm pretty sure you inhaled them all."

"Look, some of us were here for a while and were hungry. We had to work ourselves up for the interrogation."

"Intervention," Cor called from the other room.

"That was the least dramatic interro-vention I've ever seen," Liam said. "I thought there'd be a little more by way of accusations and general shock."

"How dare you get me pregnant," I said, jostling against him.

He rolled his eyes. "I meant accusations at you."

"You got him pregnant." Aislin pointed at Liam while her eyes sparkled. "Oh god, this is going to be so much fun with you two together."

"Hmm, maybe I'm regretting all of this now," Liam said, trying to tug away from me.

I squeezed him tighter against me. "No escape, no escape."

Declan let out a snort. "I have no sympathy. You knew what you were in for."

The kitchen table was covered with the remains of cinnamon rolls, a half-eaten plate of bacon, and a breakfast casserole that had already been torn into. But there were biscuits too, and honestly, I didn't even care what was left to eat. I was so fucking happy just to be here with the love of my life, surrounded by my family.

Josie had gotten along with my family, and we'd made it work the best we could for years, but lingering tension had always existed. Turned out all the arguments and general lack of cohesion had been signs we weren't right for each other.

Because this, with Liam? I wasn't trying to make anything work. We just did. The sense of rightness settled into my veins, lifting me higher than I'd experienced before.

"Okay, how slowly are you going to eat that cinnamon roll?" Rory started arguing with Aislin again. "It's like you're fucking taunting me."

I nuzzled against the side of Liam's neck. "I love you," I whispered in his ear. "More than I ever thought possible."

The way his whole body melted against mine told me all I needed to know, but he whispered those words back.

"I love you too, Ollie. For as long as you'll have me."

Little did he know, I was planning on forever.

Chapter Nineteen

Liam

It hadn't even been a week since dealing with whatever the attempt at an interrogation had been at the Brannon household before we were facing the next group of nosy bitches who wanted answers. In other words, my friends.

I went to game nights at Kelsey, Ruby, and Marco's place pretty regularly, but Maeve had been extra insistent I attend this one with my new boyfriend. She hadn't gotten to see us together, since my ass had been overnighting at Ollie's house most of the week, which I had the feeling would be a trend more and more while we were together. Not only because Ollie was needy as hell but also because he brought out the same in me. But with him, that didn't scare me.

"What are we going to play tonight?" Ollie asked, slinging an arm around my shoulders as we approached the front door.

"Aren't you worried about coming out to my friends?" I asked. How had he been so chill throughout most of this? The only bit of tension I'd seen from him was when he needed to tell his family everything, but even that had been a blip. However, I shouldn't have been surprised. That had always been Ollie. If a curveball came his way, he'd just flow with it and find the silver lining—the opposite of my grumpy ass.

It was one of the things I loved most about him.

"Why?" Ollie shrugged. "They already know we're together now, and most of them are queer."

"Fine, be rational." I twisted the doorknob and entered. I'd never come here with a boyfriend before, but there was a weird mixture of comfort with the new since I had dragged Ollie along in the past. Except now he was all mine.

That reality had barely settled in, despite the amount of time we spent together, how often we fucked, and waking up in his bed with his body wrapped around me every morning. I'd been dreaming of this for so long that I felt like I was still walking through one.

We wandered into the hallway, loud voices making it clear everyone had gathered around the gaming table in their living room like always. My skin prickled in anticipation. Not like I hadn't let my friends in, but this part of me had always been shielded from the world at large. Now I was exposed wherever we went because I melted over almost everything Ollie did or said. Unless it was fucking ridiculous because I still rolled my eyes as much as I always did. To be fair, all the Brannons were ridiculous.

The moment we stepped into view, Maeve's eyes met mine from her spot at the end of the table. "Look who's showed up," Maeve said loudly and bolted from her seat.

I braced myself for the whirlwind.

She slammed into both of us, a feat for such a small human, and threw her arms around us. "I'm so happy for both of you."

My throat thickened at the seriousness from my ever-snarky best friend. "Thank you," I said, my words coming out a little shaky.

When she pulled away, her bright eyes glistened a little. "Come on, fuckfaces, we've been waiting for you to bust out Blood Rage."

And that was the Maeve I'd expected. I sucked in a breath to push back my annoying emotions and walked up to the others. Word had spread that Ollie and I were coming tonight together, so everyone had turned out for game night, which was a rarity. By this time, Sammy, aka the toddler of perpetual chaos, was down for the evening, which left the adults free to game.

Cole and Lex were hanging out with Kelsey and Ruby on the couches while Marco, Theo, and Rhys all waited at the table, the game set out already.

"Before they get dragged into intense gaming mode, I want the official introduction," Ruby said. She sat up from her comfortable spot with her head on Kelsey's lap where her girlfriend had been playing with her dark, wavy hair.

"Fine," I said, gesturing to Ollie. "Look, this is a guy you've clearly never met before in your life—since he hasn't been over here a million times before."

Ollie slid behind me and wrapped his arms around me as if he tried to engulf my body in a single move. I leaned back against his chest. "Hey, I finally got my head out of my ass and realized Liam's the love of my life, and we're going to spend every day together swooning and staring into each other's eyes—"

I clapped my hand over his mouth, stopping him from embarrassing me further. I might love the man to pieces, but right now he was being a pain in my ass. "We're boyfriends. Introductions complete."

"I don't know," Lex said, his grin widening. "I want to hear more of what Ollie was saying."

"No, you don't. You just want to watch me suffer."

"Of course he does. He's a sadist," Theo called out from over at the table.

"Sounds familiar," Marco said, casting a glance at Ruby. Kelsey snickered, only to squeak a moment later when Ruby pinched her thigh.

These people. Warmth flooded my chest, even as I attempted to keep myself from not being a total sap while having Ollie's arms wrapped around me. He felt so warm, so comfortable, like a favorite hoodie in the fall, and I wanted to bask in this bliss we'd found. The casual affection he doled upon me in heaps made me say "fuck it" to my normal ways because he was too sweet to resist. Nothing like my surly ass.

"Does anyone need to grill me or anything? Threaten me?" Ollie asked, all earnest and shit.

I shook my head, the corner of my lips quirking in a grin.

"Nah, Liam's capable of fending for himself," Rhys said.

"Grill you about what? We know you," Theo said. The gleam in his gaze conveyed how happy he was for me. Theo and Maeve were the two who had been aware of my crush the longest, even though I'd never told anyone I'd been pining for my best friend for over a decade.

"Congratulations, guys," Cole said. "I'm really happy for you both."

"Thanks," Ollie said, pressing a kiss against the side of my head, all the affection like a sugar overload.

"If we're going to dawdle before the game, I'm grabbing a beer." Maeve walked toward the kitchen. She snagged my gaze and tilted her head.

"I'll come with," I said, slipping from Ollie's grasp. I gave him a quick kiss on his cheek. "Can you grab us seats?"

"Absolutely, baby," he replied, and a chorus of coos sounded from around the room. I flipped my middle finger at them. Maeve had orchestrated my escape, and I wouldn't waste the chance to sneak out of the limelight for a few moments.

When I stepped into the kitchen, I sucked in a sigh of relief. Being the center of attention might not faze Ollie, but that was because he'd grown up in chaos. Around the Brannons, I could watch the antics from the sidelines and chime in occasionally, which was more my speed. This, on the other hand, was him spending more time with my best friends, which meant all that focus turned my way.

"I'm shocked you emerged from the love nest," Maeve said as she grabbed two beers from the fridge and set them on the counter. "Let me guess. You two have been going hot and heavy from the second you popped that top?"

"Ha, funny," I said, my tone dry as usual. Though she wasn't wrong, and my cheeks warmed a little at all the filthy things we'd been up to. The amount of time I spent with Ollie's cock in my mouth or ass was nothing short of blissful and fulfilled fantasies I hadn't dared entertain in the past.

"This is serious, though." She lowered her voice. "Right? Like moving-in serious?"

"We haven't talked about it yet."

"But we both know that's where it's going." She gave me a cavalier grin that wobbled. I closed the distance between us and crushed her in a hug. Maeve's pointy little chin burrowed into my shoulder as she tried to squeeze the life out of me. Apart from Ollie, she was my best damn friend, and we'd lived together for so long now. I'd been avoiding change for a long time, just stuck in a holding pattern.

Existing at a job when I knew I could do better, sticking with one-night stands instead of trying for anything real, pining after my best friend who'd been married at the time.

Except the moment Ollie and I got together, change filtered in—not in an aggressive way like a tidal wave but more like the tide itself, lapping up to the shore. It infiltrated—first with my relationship with Ollie until it affected the rest of my life as well. Ollie loved having me in his house, and he made that abundantly clear. And he'd also started helping me with the paperwork to get my business going so I could quit my toxic job.

However, I wouldn't have reached any of these turning points without the people in this house—especially Maeve.

"Hey," I said, realizing what needed to be said. We finally pulled apart so I could look her in the eye. "Even if I move in with Ollie, I'm not abandoning our friendship. You're too damn important to me."

She fiddled with the top of her beer bottle. "Well, I guess someone is going to need to force you out of the love nest to socialize so you don't become feral."

A laugh burst from my chest, even as my heart squeezed tight. Moving out into Ollie's place was my future. I knew that, just like I'd always known I would open my own practice, no matter how much I resisted. Change had been my nemesis for a long, long while, but until recently, I hadn't understood that embracing it was the best way through life.

The sole way to claim what incredible moments you possibly could.

"I'll go feral if I don't have you dragging me out to coffee shops or game nights, so please don't stop."

Her bright eyes got a wicked gleam I had the feeling I'd regret. "Excellent. I'm going to remind you of this moment anytime you complain about going out. 'Oh, Maeve, but being around people is the worst.' 'Oh, Maeve, I want to hide away and become a cave troll.'"

Her high-pitched whining sounded nothing like me, and I flicked her in the arm. A laugh exploded out of her, and she slid the other beer bottle my way. She nabbed an opener from the trio's display of barware on the far wall of the kitchen and opened both of ours.

She lifted her bottle, and we clinked.

"To you and Ollie. I'm happy you finally got your guy. Now let's get this game night started."

"I see how it is," I said as I followed her into the living room. "You just want me around to make sure we've got a good headcount for board games."

"Duh," she shot back, eyes twinkling. "Who else am I going to get to play Gloomhaven with me?"

"Definitely not me," Rhys called out. "I don't have the attention span for that game."

"Few do," Lex said.

Ollie already sat at the table, an open seat next to him saved for me. It was a sight I'd seen in the past a million times, yet now that we were together, it hit differently. His gorgeous brown eyes crinkled with a smile just for me, and warmth flooded through my whole body. I memorized every little detail from his broad shoulders straining the fabric of his Brannon Contractors work tee to the trimmed beard I liked to run my fingers through while he thrust into me. The tattoos I'd traced with my tongue, the thick thighs I'd seen flex—hell, everything about him drove me wild.

And he was all mine.

I wasn't sure if I'd ever be able to get over that fact. I wasn't sure I wanted to.

I slid into the spot beside him, and he pressed a sweet kiss to the side of my neck, the kind that made me shiver. I was aware our friends were watching, but I didn't care about guarding myself anymore. I was so incandescently happy, more than I thought I could feel.

As our fingers laced underneath the table, our love out in the open for everyone to see, I knew I'd spend the rest of my life loving this man.

Some part of me had understood for a long time—he'd always been the one.

Epilogue

Ollie

Six Months Later

"**B**abe, if you don't hurry up, we're going to be late for your divorce party," Liam called from the front of our house. He'd lasted a month before caving to my incessant begging for him to move in with me, as it should be.

Little did he know we were definitely going to be late.

I slipped my hand into my pocket, my fingers brushing against the box I'd snuck there from the top drawer of my dresser. The past six months had been the best damn ones of my life. The heights I rose to in my relationship with Liam just proved that he was the one I should've been with all along, and I didn't want to waste a second more. Together, we were stronger than ever.

Business was going great, with Dad handing more and more of the reins to Cor and me, and Liam had finalized his business plan for his physical therapy practice, got the loan, and quit his soul-sucking job. He planned on opening the Motion Clinic next year, and I was so fucking thrilled for him. Between my demanding family and his demanding friend group, it felt like we were always busy, but I was dating Liam, which meant he always made sure we had time by ourselves too.

Whether we were going on ridiculous birding dates, kicking back to game together, or fucking each other's brains out, we meshed in every way possible. He was my soulmate—there was no doubt about it in my mind.

And today, I wanted him to know that for sure.

I stepped into the entryway where Liam waited, my palms beginning to sweat a little.

His blond hair was swept to the side, and the slight bit of scruff on his chin added to the strong line of his jaw. Those blue eyes of his were devastatingly gorgeous, and between his strong nose and sensuous lips, the lower one always a little more plump than the top, he was the most stunning person I'd ever seen. He wore a green button-down far too well with black jeans that highlighted his perfect peach of an ass, and I wanted to flip him over and take a bite. He'd grabbed his jacket, since the February weather was brisk and unfriendly, even though we'd only be out in the cold for a few minutes.

"Before we go." I approached him slowly. "There's something I wanted to ask you."

Liam furrowed his brow, and I could already see his beautiful mind in motion, troubleshooting problems that hadn't arrived yet.

I stopped in front of him and reached into my pocket. When I started to lower onto one knee, Liam's expression shifted, his eyes widening.

Nerves rushed through me in a fierce sweep, but there was no backing down now. Maybe he'd think this was too early, but in my mind, this was long overdue. I pulled out the ring I'd bought a month ago and looked into the eyes of the man I loved.

"Liam Kelly," I said, my voice trembling. Fuck, I hadn't been nearly this nervous when I'd asked Josie. Then again she hadn't been the right one for me. "You've been by my side for most of my life. My partner in crime for all the stupid shit I've gotten into, the first person I've always gone to when I was upset, and the one who knows how to cheer me up without even trying. The competent way you navigate any hurdles, how you're prickly for everyone else but soft for me—I'm so in love with you. Each day is better because you're mine, but that's not enough. I want the rest of our lives together. Marry me?"

Liam stared back at me, his blue eyes glazed over.

I swallowed hard, suddenly unsure as to what he'd say. Before I could ask, Liam dropped to his knees in front of me and brought his mouth to mine. I cupped the side of his face as I kissed him back with the same ferocity roaring through my veins. He tasted like mint and felt like fire, and each sweet, intoxicating kiss from him was like our first.

I sank into the heady swirl that arrived with his mouth on mine, how he managed to electrify the air around us. We kissed hard, all tongues and teeth, until we slowed to long, lingering kisses that sent waves of pleasure through me. When he finally pulled back, his shoulders were heaving and his expression was soft and open, the sort he reserved for me alone.

"I'd love nothing more," he whispered. "You've always been the only man for me."

I tugged the ring from the box and slipped it onto his finger. "Well, it's about time the rest of the world knows it."

Liam arched his eyebrow, a sexy little move I loved. "I'm pretty sure they're all aware. You don't exactly make your intentions quiet."

"Yeah, but I bet they won't realize this divorce party is going to be an engagement party." I stared at my ring on Liam's finger. My heart swelled so large it felt separate from my body—mostly because it was. It had always been his, even when I hadn't been aware.

"We'll see," Liam said, a broad grin stretching his lips. "Come on now. Let's get to your party." He tugged me up, and after a short scramble for my keys, wallet, and coat, I led the way out the door to my car. The entire way there, Liam was beaming, and hell, I wanted to beat my chest in pride at putting that expression on my face.

"Ready to be a Brannon?" I asked as we settled into my Jeep for the couple minute drive over to my folks.

Liam rolled his eyes, and I started the ignition and set off down the road.

"Why couldn't you become a Kelly?" he challenged.

"Because your family doesn't care if I do whereas my family would murder me for changing the family name," I argued as we veered onto the familiar street to my parents' house. "Besides, we already adopted your family awhile ago."

"You all are a special breed," Liam said, the amused tone warming me up from the inside out.

"That you're knowingly marrying into," I pointed out. "So that must make you just as crazy as the rest of us." I pulled to a park in front of my parents' place, which was littered with cars. We might be one of the last to arrive to my divorce party, but the reason was definitely worth it.

"Maybe I am," Liam said, and the soft way he stared at me from the passenger's seat made me melt all over again. I wanted to scoop him into my arms and carry him inside, but I'd settle for kissing the fuck out of him and holding his hand. I leaned in and stole a fierce kiss that left us both breathless, and then we exited the car.

Our fingers wove together because as I'd always suspected, my sometimes surly best friend was as much of a touch slut as me. Besides my siblings, we'd invited Liam's family and the friends I'd always considered Liam's but who I'd become close as hell with in the last six months. Which meant the house would be packed tight with people—but they were the exact ones we wanted to share the good news with.

When we reached the door, I flashed him a grin. "Ready for the chaos?"

He offered me a lopsided smile that made my heart thump a little harder. "With you? Always."

Liam tugged the door open.

The wall of noise slammed into me at once. We stepped in through the entrance.

"Look who finally arrived at his own party," Rory called out . He was sitting on the couch with Kelsey, Ruby, and Marco. My brother had a backward baseball cap on, covering his thick, dark hair, and he was holding Ruby's forearm like he examined her tattoo.

"Wait, Ollie's here? Does that mean we can have cake now?" Rhys said, mid-stumble while he chased Sammy across the living room floor. Rhys's hair was a mess, and his clothes were rumpled like he'd taken several tumbles.

"For you or the kiddo?" Cole asked, an amused smirk on his lips.

"Me, obviously," Rhys said. Sammy let out a loud squeal, evading his dad again.

"Oh, we were supposed to save that cake?" Aislin said, poking her head in from the kitchen.

"Stop eating all the fucking desserts," Rory yelled back.

"Sweet thing like this? Makes perfect sense," Maeve said in her flirty tone as she rested a hand on Aislin's shoulder. I heaved a sigh. That would be a headache in the making if Maeve was on the prowl.

"Don't let her deceive you." Declan strode past Maeve and Aislin. "There's nothing sweet about my sister."

"Rude," Aislin shot back as she leaned in a little closer to Maeve's inviting arms.

"Yeah, we better put a kibosh on that," Liam muttered into my ear.

"I've got an easy way." I lifted our intertwined hands. "Hey, everyone. I've got an announcement."

"Putting us at the center of attention wasn't what I had in mind," Liam whisper-hissed as everyone stared at us.

Cor popped in from the other room, with Mom and Dad hot on his heels. "Oh look, Ollie's engaged again."

I opened my mouth and shut it again. All eyes were glued on us, and more than a few folks had zeroed in on the platinum band gleaming around Liam's finger.

"Holy shit, seriously?" Maeve stepped away from my sister and bolted toward us, her red hair flying.

"What happened?" Theo came from the kitchen too, followed by Lex—which meant there were far, far too many people in my parents' living room, but I wouldn't have it any other way.

Mom and Dad stepped up to us first and wrapped us in big hugs before I could blink.

"I'm so happy for you," Mom whispered in my ear. "It's clear he was always the one for you."

"You two are a perfect match," Dad said, squeezing Liam's shoulder again.

"What's going on?" Liam's mom and dad came around the corner where my folks had been. Liam was the spitting image of his mother from the light blond hair and expressive blue eyes to the same slender jaw. His father had softer blue eyes and dark brown hair, as well as a stockier frame than his son. Liam's parents were quieter types, which made it clear where Liam had gotten his chill from, but both were always kind and humored my family's insanity.

"Ollie and Liam are getting married," Cor said. "Because my brother has a hard-on for commitment."

"Ignore him," Mom said. "We're thrilled."

Before I could prepare myself, we were swept into a rush of hugs and congratulations from our friends and family, but I made sure I was glued to Liam's side the whole time. Shouts, cheers, and laughter rang through the room, and I got jostled and slapped on the back as much as I got hugged. My heart thumped so hard it might burst out of my chest, but the sight of Liam as my fiancé amid all our loved ones? Yeah, I couldn't picture anything better. Flat-out pandemonium lasted for at least fifteen minutes straight before the crowd began to disperse. We'd barely made it steps from the entrance in all that time, so I stepped up next to Liam and wrapped my arms around his shoulders again to drag him against me.

"That was an experience," he said, a rueful grin on his face. "You understand that after this, I'll be peopled out for weeks, right?"

"Good. We can just fuck nonstop the whole time."

A delicious little shiver traveled through Liam, one I wanted to bottle up and save.

"You realize you're still close enough that I can hear," Declan said, giving me an unamused look. "Are we having cake or not?"

"I've got cake every day." Lex waggled his brows. Theo let out a beleaguered sigh.

"You're not wrong," Marco said, passing a glance in Theo's direction, and Ruby snickered.

"Mama, want cake." Sammy leapt onto Kelsey's lap while Rhys collapsed onto the floor, clearly exhausted.

"All right, all right," I said, gesturing everyone to the kitchen. "Let's get this cake thing started before we have a riot on our hands."

"With this family, I wouldn't be surprised." Mom drifted past us with Dad in tow as the majority of the party migrated into the kitchen. Cole dipped down next to Rhys on the couch while Ruby and Marco helped Kelsey scramble after Sammy, who was en route to the kitchen on a mission for sugar. Lex was whispering something in Theo's ear that made him blush like crazy over by the loveseat, and Maeve and my sister had vanished, which I still didn't trust.

The chaos of our large group of friends and family combined made my heart glow—all the bickering, the love, the wild ups and downs. However, that paled in comparison to the way I felt about the man by my side.

The one who'd promised to be with me for the rest of our lives.

I leaned in and pressed a kiss to Liam's temple. "Thank you," I said, the depth of those words settling deep inside my soul.

"For what?" Liam asked.

"Waiting for me. Loving me." I gave a helpless little shrug. "I don't know how else to explain it, but you're my person. You always have been."

He sank against me, and I drew in the spicy scent of his cologne that always made my pulse quicken. His eyes were unwavering as he responded. "And you've always been mine."

Together we stood for a moment, basking in all the changes that had occurred in such a short time since I got divorced. We'd spent years in stasis, neither of us willing to shift out of our situations, yet the past six months had been a total metamorphosis. I'd found my path with stronger footing than ever, with the right person by my side, and Liam walked confidently beside me every step of the way.

The truth had finally reached me after so many years running from it. Change was terrifying, breathless, and inevitable.

However, it was also the only way to grow.

He was a fresh sunrise on my horizon every day, and I wanted to spend the rest of my life changing with Liam as we explored whatever the future had in store for us.

I had no doubt our adventure would be unforgettable.

Afterword

Thank you for reading Liam and Ollie's book, the end of the Hot Under the Collar series. If you're craving more though, never fear—the Brannon Boys will be here in 2025! More low angst blue collar adventures will be coming with Cormac, Declan, and Rory, and it's going to be all the same vibes as Hot Under the Collar with regular appearances from the characters you know and love.

I have to take a moment and gush about what this series did for me and my writing. While I still adore hurt/comfort and third person romances with my whole heart, which I get to play with in the Dungeons and Dating universe, there was something freeing about writing first person low angst for me and playing around with more comedic writing. I've always thought it was something I couldn't do, but lo and behold, I ended up loving it, which is why I'm going to be splashing around with the Hot Under the Collar universe for a whole lot longer.

Thank you guys for diving in and sticking around for the whole ride. Strap in, because there's so much more to come!

If you enjoyed the book, leave a review. Kind words are what us authors survive on, and I can tell you personally I treasure each and every one.

Also By

This might be the end of the Hot Under the Collar series, but there's more to come in that universe!

Ready for more with the Brannon Boys?

Heat Transfer (Brannon Boys #1) is coming January 2025!

Cor's crush on the straight boy in sword fighting class has been unrequited, but with one crossed sword, that's all about to change...

Cor

From the second I showed up for sword fighting class, Felix grabbed my attention. Yet not only was he straight, but he also had a girlfriend. However, the more we hang, the more I can't help but hang on his every word, every look. And when he ends up newly single, I can't stop my hopes from running rampant.

Felix

I've been accused of talking about my best friend Cor too much, but when my client mistakes us for boyfriends and invites us to the historical gala of our dreams...well, it's time to ask him to be my fake date. Except fake dating Cor doesn't just feel natural, it feels better than most relationships I've been in. And when my curiosity for more takes the wheel, we end up exploring everything.

We're circling each other, just like we do in a sword fighting match, however, this isn't just skill or reputation on the line. Far too fast, it becomes clear that I love him, and if he doesn't feel the same, I won't just be disarmed—losing him would deliver the finishing blow.

Also By

Want hurt/comfort romances featuring a geeky, queer found family?
Read across the rainbow with the Dungeons and Dating series today!

Strength Check (Dungeons and Dating #1):

Roller derby, board games, and love collide in this roommates to lovers romance.

Wisdom Check (Dungeons and Dating #2):

Julian's boss is newly single, ridiculously hot, and looking his way. He's so screwed.

Intelligence Check (Dungeons and Dating #3):

Mason gives people too many chances, Hunter gives too few, but are they willing to take a chance on each other?

Constitution Check (Dungeons and Dating #4):

One night was all Kelly promised. One night was all Tabby offered. And yet one night wasn't nearly enough...

Dexterity Check (Dungeons and Dating #5):

Eli's sworn off irresponsible flirts, and Arjun's one of the worst—aggravating, provoking, and everything Eli can't resist.

Charisma Check (Dungeons and Dating #6):

Never fall for the straight guy—Jasper knows better. At least until his straight guy crush starts crushing back...

Also By

Ready to turn up the heat? Dive into the Leather and Lattes universe!

Immersion Play (Leather and Lattes #1)
One bratty boy searching for somewhere to call home, one damaged Daddy Dom looking to escape his grief, and one kinky found family ready to help them both heal.
Extraction Play (Leather and Lattes #2)
Pixie is off limits, yet Eva can't seem to stay away from her brother's best friend...

About the Author

Katherine McIntyre is a feisty chick with a big attitude despite her short stature. She writes stories featuring snarky women, ragtag crews, and men with bad attitudes—high chance for a passionate speech thrown into the mix. As a genderqueer geek who's always stepped to her own beat, she's made it her mission to write stories that represent the broad spectrum of people out there. Easily distracted by cats and sugar.

Made in the USA
Middletown, DE
04 January 2025